To Wed His Christmas Lady
The Brethren Series

For more information about the author:
www.christicaldwellauthor.com
christicaldwellauthor@gmail.com
Twitter: @ChristiCaldwell
Or on Facebook at: Christi Caldwell Author

For first glimpse at covers, excerpts, and free bonus material, be sure to sign up for my monthly newsletter!
Printed in the USA.

Cover Design and Interior Format

To
Wed His
Christmas Lady

Heart
of a
Duke

THE
SERIES

USA TODAY BESTSELLER

CHRISTI
CALDWELL

OTHER TITLES BY
CHRISTI CALDWELL

THE HEART OF A SCANDAL

In Need of a Knight—Prequel Novella

Schooling the Duke

Heart of a Duke

In Need of a Duke—Prequel Novella

For Love of the Duke

More than a Duke

The Love of a Rogue

Loved by a Duke

To Love a Lord

The Heart of a Scoundrel

To Wed His Christmas Lady

To Trust a Rogue

The Lure of a Rake

To Woo a Widow

LORDS OF HONOR

Seduced by a Lady's Heart

Captivated by a Lady's Charm

Rescued by a Lady's Love

Tempted by a Lady's Smile

SCANDALOUS SEASONS

Forever Betrothed, Never the Bride

Never Courted, Suddenly Wed

Always Proper, Suddenly Scandalous

Always a Rogue, Forever Her Love

A Marquess for Christmas

Once a Wallflower, at Last His Love

CHAPTER 1

William James Alexander Winchester Hargrove, I expect you home for the Christmastide Season! Your mother and I (but particularly your mother), have expectations for you.

Post Script

Your mother wanted me to stress that we are expecting you home prior to Christmas.

~Your father

Just outside Farnham, England
December, 1817

WILLIAM HARGROVE, THE MARQUESS OF Grafton, *should* have learned early on to be wary of barters presented by his father, the Duke of Billingsley.

At just six years of age, his father had dangled one of Cook's Shrewsbury cakes in exchange for William's beloved toy soldiers. With a boy's impulsivity, William handed over every last figure from colonel to captain. Only after, when sugar flaked his cheeks and lips and the treat was gone, and his father's large palm extended out, empty, he'd discovered for the first time—one always came out on the losing end of Father's deals. William had turned over his toys forever for a bite of cake. It was a permanent loss in exchange for a fleeting pleasure.

That had been the first barter William had made with the clever duke.

The one he'd made as a youth of eighteen had been William's last. The problem of making a pledge when one was but eighteen years of age was that time seems endless and years were eternal when you're nothing more than a boy. A black curse ripped from his lips.

But now, he'd run out of time.

With snow falling about him, William leaned against the mighty oak and again skimmed the contents of his father's missive. The note could not be clearer had the words been written: *Your travels are up. It is time to see to your duty.* His stomach muscles tightened. For that last deal struck would prove the most final in terms of what he'd sacrificed for eight fleeting years—his freedom.

As boisterous in real life as he was upon the page, the duke fit not at all with rigid Societal expectations of and for a duke. William's earliest memories of his father included the man's booming laughter as he'd raced the length of the ballroom with William seated precariously upon his shoulders. Still…for that warmth and affection, his father was a duke in every sense of the word. As such, there was, and always had been, the great expectation that William would do right by the Billingsley line as deemed right by his loving sire.

As a young man of eighteen, in exchange for a pledge to wed the spoiled, cold, and rotten daughter of the Duke of Ravenscourt, his father had granted William eight years of freedom. Freedom to travel. To explore. And to come and go as though the dukedom would not one day pass to him.

Why hadn't he insisted on more time? His lips twisted with bitterness. Then, a handful more years could never have been enough. Nor did his desires have anything to do with the wanderlust that had filled him in his youth. After years of traveling, the prospect of returning to England and his family was a potent one. Or it should be. Not now. Not when presented with the grim future awaiting him. And where that inevitability was one expected of all noblemen, it was not a matter of giving up his freedom—but rather, *whom* he'd give his freedom up to. For the woman his parents would bind William to was colder than the snow that even now stung his skin. And while such matches with those frosty, emotionless ladies were commonplace in polite Society, his own parents' union had stood as testament to the possibility of more—love and warmth and affection.

William clenched his hands reflexively about the page and the vellum crackled noisily in the winter quiet. His mount, Thunder, loosely tied to the opposite tree, picked up his head. The horse flicked his ears and nervously danced about. "Easy," he soothed, and that seemed to have some kind of calming effect for the black Friesian. Redirecting his attention out once more, William stared into the distant gray-white horizon. He fixed his gaze down the snow-covered, old, Roman road that would inevitably lead him home.

He gritted his teeth, hating his damn foolish younger self who'd sacrificed any hope of a marriage based on anything more than a cold, emotionless, business arrangement between two powerful families.

A gust of wind whipped the steady, winter snow in his eyes and stung his cheeks. Dread pitted his stomach. It was time for him to wed. With a curse that would have burned his mother's ears, he crumpled the note into a ball, stalked to the edge of the road, and hurled the sheet into the wind.

The growing storm captured that loathsome summons and whipped it up into the air. He stared, numb, as the ivory vellum fell to the earth, and then was carried by the wind, onward—until it disappeared.

If only I could do the same.

But he couldn't. He'd been wandering for years, away from the world where he would someday ascend to the lofty title of duke. And more, he'd been wandering away from *her*.

"Lady Clarisse Falcot." His lip peeled back in a snarl. The ever so proper lady his parents would see him wed. He balled his hands at his sides. His father had, of course, known just what to dangle before his adventure-craving son's grasp—the ability to travel.

A hungering filled him to turn on his heel, mount Thunder, and ride off in the opposite direction. For the sliver of an instant he allowed himself that possibility, but then thrust it aside. He was a man who, at the very least, honored his word. Where was the comfort in that? William skimmed his gaze over the lightly snow-covered countryside and easily found that loathsome ivory vellum, now a wrinkled ball, tumbling over the white snow. Periodically, the increasing wind carried the page further away. Only, disposing of that missive would not undo the pledge he'd made that would ultimately join him to that miserable brat he'd had the displeasure of knowing as a child.

After effectively burying the thought of her all these years, he let the memories of her slip in. He'd known his mother's god-daughter, Lady Clarisse Falcot, since she was in the nursery and he'd been a mere boy of ten. He recalled the precise moment he'd known Clarisse was no manner of woman he'd ever wed, despite his father's clear expectations. On a visit to her family's properties, he'd stepped into the foyer. She'd been a girl but had the servants lined up. With a frigid tone better reserved for Wellington himself in the heart of battle, she'd ordered them about in search of some bauble or trinket. He'd stood frozen in the entrance of the duke's country home, alongside his family, and a chill had snaked through him to rival the current storm. *This would be the girl my father will someday bind me to?*

Their gazes had caught and she'd stared at him through nar-rowed, angry eyes. And he'd despised her from the start. Cold, icy, and rude to the servants. As a girl of ten, she was the epitome of pompous nobility. His father had ingrained into William early on that a man's merit came not in his birthright, but in his *sense* of right and strength of convictions. Yet, still with that, he'd wed Wil-liam off to that coldhearted, English miss who'd treated servants as though their only purpose was to serve her.

Another gust of wind whipped the steady snow into his face, stinging his cheeks. He strode over to his mount and freed Thun-der's reins from the oak tree. William climbed astride and then nudged his horse forward, onward toward his family's country seat in Farnham. Through the worsening conditions, he struggled to see into the tempest. He guided his mount onward, along the snow-covered, old, Roman roads, and struggled to see through the curtain of heavy white flakes.

Momentarily blinded, William slowed Thunder to a walk, mindful of the winds gusting small drifts on the rough roads. It was inevitable. Lady Clarisse could not have stayed a girl forever. And by the whispers and gossip he'd heard before he'd begun his journey home from London, she'd grown into a shrewish, foul extension of her younger self and the duke who'd sired her.

He pulled on the reins and stared about at the desolate landscape painted white by nature's brushstroke. Thunder shifted nervously under him.

Mind in tumult, William looked down the path toward his family's estate, that family who even now awaited his arrival. Thunder danced beneath him as he contemplated the two paths. One home. The other toward the inn a short distance back that would offer refuge from the storm and a temporary reprieve from his inevitable fate.

William doffed his hat and shook the flakes from the brim. He promptly placed his cap back on and pulled it low to shield his eyes from the snow. Yes, he must return. And yet, his family could not expect him to return in the midst of an increasingly violent storm, even if Christmas was but days away.

He cast a last reluctant look down the road leading to Farnham and his family—and his future—and then, decision made, urged Thunder back toward the Fox and Hare Inn. He shoved aside the needling of guilt. There would be time enough for a reunion after the storm.

A SHORT WHILE LATER, WILLIAM DISMOUNTED before the modest inn. Wind whipped the large, wood sign back and forth, while the howling wind stretched across the land. He wrapped the horse's reins around his hand and led him back to the stables. With each step, his boots sank quietly into the thick blanket of snow. He stopped outside the stable and rapped several times.

Silence met his knocking. With a frown, he glanced about and then banged again, this time harder. The door opened and a man nearly one foot smaller than William's own six-foot four-inch frame looked up at him. The wizened figure squinted through thick lenses. "Do you need something?"

The wind wailed about them. "I am looking for a stable for my horse until the storm lets up." Or forever, would be preferable if it meant he did not have to return to the responsibilities he'd put off all these years.

The hostler collected the reins and guided his mount into the stables.

"Thank—" The old man slammed the stable door closed in his face. "—you," he finished wryly, and then ducking his head to shield his face from the specks of icy snow hitting him, he returned down the snowy path to the front of the inn.

Other noblemen might chafe at being treated with such disrespect. William grinned. There was, and always had been, something freeing in traveling about without being hindered by a title or ancestry. To the world at large, he'd been just William.

William reached the old inn he'd passed many times before and shoved the door open. He stepped inside and blinked several times in an attempt to bring the dimly lit space into focus. His boots dripping water on the already stained hardwood floors, William closed the door behind him. The blaring storm warred with the quiet in the empty inn. But for the hiss and crack of the blazing fire, silence raged. He skimmed his gaze about the darkened room.

From the corner of the establishment, a bleating snore rent the stillness of the room. A man sat at the back corner table with his white head buried on his hands.

The quick shuffle of footsteps called his attention to an old woman making her way down the stairs. "There is someone here, Martin," she shouted.

The white-haired man jerked awake. "What?" He looked frantically about. "Who?"

The old woman stopped at the base of the stairs and eyed William as he shrugged out of his modest cloak. She looked him over. Her gaze lingered on his coarse garments better suited to a man who worked with his hands than an heir to a dukedom and a frown turned her lips. "We have a patron," she said and then came over to collect his garment.

With a murmur of thanks, he turned it over to her and rolled his shoulders. "I am in need of rooms. Do you have any available?"

The man he took to be her husband snorted. "We have all three rooms available for the Christmastide season." William could practically see the wheels of the old innkeeper's mind turning as he calculated the coin to be had with any guest, in light of their previous zero patrons. "Will you be staying the night?"

A noisy wind slammed into the establishment. Ice and snow rattled the ancient windowpanes. "I will be staying until the storm passes." Though in actuality, when faced with the prospect of returning home, staying forever in the modest, cold, and blessedly empty inn seemed far preferable.

CHAPTER 2

THE CARRIAGE WAS NOT COMING.

Somewhere between the departure of the first carriage and the seventh, Lady Clarisse Falcot, daughter to the Duke of Ravenscourt, had resolved herself to that eventuality.

Except, standing in the corner of her chambers at Mrs. Belden's Finishing School staring down as the *eighth* carriage pulled away she readily admitted, only to herself, that one could not truly be resolved to being forgotten—at the Christmastide season, no less—by one's father.

In the crystal pane, partially frosted from the winter's cold, a bitter smile twisted the corner of her lips. She tightened her grip upon the cherished heart pendant in her hands so that the crimson ruby bit painfully into her palm.

Then, what purpose did she truly serve to the man, more stranger than sire, beyond increasing his power and wealth? This latest, glaring indignity was only one more reminder of her absolute and total lack of worth to the duke.

There is little use to me of a girl…the only purpose you'll serve is as a match with Billingsley's son…if he ever brings himself 'round to returning from his gallivanting…

Her temporary chambers here at Mrs. Belden's echoed under the force of that remembered laughter.

The soft shuffle of footsteps at the entrance of the room pulled her attention away from the lead windowpane as her lady's maid,

Alison hurried into the room. She caught Cara's gaze and a blush stained the young woman's cheeks. "My lady," she murmured. Did the girl suspect that her mistress had been forgotten? Pity filled the girl's eyes. "I am sure the carriage will arrive shortly."

Cara wanted to spew all kinds of cold responses about the insolence of the woman's supposition. Except, shame slapped at her cheeks as Alison set to packing the final trunk. She rushed about the room, pointedly averting her gaze. Jagged humiliation lanced her and the muscles of her throat tightened. Only this maelstrom of emotions cutting off her ability to breathe was about more than embarrassment.

Pain.

Cara yanked her attention back to the window as her mind wrapped around that one word. She balled and unballed her hands at her sides. The cold pendant in her grasp dug sharply into her palm and she welcomed that diversionary sting of discomfort. For years, she'd built fortresses about herself, protecting her from that pain; hating the emotion as much as she hated the man her father was. Pain was a sentiment that had weakened her in ways she'd tired of; she was truly tired of being weak. It earned you pity amongst the servants and snide comments from the girls you attended finishing school with. Yes, cold and indifferent was far preferable to the gut-wrenching agony that went with laying yourself open before another person.

Yet, standing there with the wind howling forlornly outside, was it possible to be anything other than gutted by the truth that your father had forgotten to send 'round the carriage to retrieve you for the Christmastide season? Yes, she'd been invisible as a girl. A powerful peer had little use in a daughter—except for the match she might someday make. And now, as a woman of eighteen, she served a material purpose—making an advantageous match with another ducal family. Still, even with that pawn-like figure she'd been transformed into by their power-driven Society, Cara was still worthless to her father, in even the most material way. Long ago, she'd accepted that. But deep inside, in the place where hope dwelled, she dreamed of a man who could love her. A man who was kind and bold and strong; who could see past the ice upon the surface and, instead, see a soul worth loving. And that man would be worth throwing over any future duke for; her sire's disapproval or any long ago signed contracts be damned.

Today's blunder on her father's part only roused the absolute foolishness in such silent yearnings. Nonetheless, a spasm wracked her heart and she rubbed her hand over her chest to dull the ache. The cold ruby of her mother's necklace pierced the fabric of her gown.

"When I am sad, my lady—"

"I am not sad," she bit out. Except, why did it feel as though she lied to the both of them? Cara shoved away such foolishness. There was little use in lamenting her father's disinterest. Regret and pain did not affection make. "Here," she thrust out her hand with the necklace—her last link to her mother, toward her waiting maid. What was the point of holding on to that cold artifact from long ago? That too-brief interlude of love had proven how fleeting and impossible that sentiment, in fact, was. "Place this in the bottom of my trunk." She didn't need the reminder of what once was. Not on this day.

A small moue of surprise formed on the maid's lips. "You are never without your necklace, my lady."

No, she was not. Cara dropped her gaze to the broken clasp of this piece that had once graced her mother's neck. Incapable of words, she shook the chain once and Alison rushed forward to claim it. The girl took in the damaged pendant and made a clucking noise like a chicken let loose. "How very sad," she said as though to herself. "'Twas a fine necklace."

The ten carat ruby and fine Italian gold had meant nothing to Cara. Rather, the memories connected to that piece as her mother had pressed it into her small hand were of far more value than any material worth attached to the necklace. "You'd still be your cheerful self with that," she said tersely, jerking her chin at the heart.

Alison blinked wildly and then a broad smile split her lips. "Oh, indeed!" She skipped over to the bed and gently wrapped the beloved piece.

It was on the tip of Cara's tongue to call for the return of that heart, but she compressed her lips into a tight line to keep from revealing that hint of weakness.

"One must always find things to be cheerful about." Her maid chatted like a magpie which, unfortunately for Cara, was often.

"There were cranberry scones for breakfast."

As respected and revered as Mrs. Belden's school was, one would never claim the headmistress' cook was in any way accomplished. "They were drier than a sack of Cook's flour."

The room trilled with Alison's laughter as she hurried from the armoire over to the open trunk at the foot of the bed. Cara winced as the young woman, between her sniffling, proceeded to carry on about the texture of the cranberries and the other parts of her breakfast meal. Cara had resolved to see her sacked the minute she'd entered into her responsibilities as maid and first smiled at her. People did not smile at her. And they decidedly did not speak to her. The maid had prattled on in a manner that had set Cara's teeth on edge. But then, the more she'd listened, the more she'd perplexedly found there was something rather *comforting* in hearing another person's voice. Oh, she'd sooner wed the miserable, pompous, future duke her father would bind her to with a smile and a "yes, please" than ever willingly admit as much. A startled laugh slipped from Cara's lips, and Alison shot a wide-eyed look back at her. Cara schooled her features and disguised that shocked sound as a cough. Alison resumed her packing, all the while humming as she went.

Yes, though Cara made it a point to not engage the girl, there was an odd solace in being with a person who spoke to you—and not *about* you. Or even, *at* you.

"Then there were the biscuits," the plump woman said crushing one of Cara's satin dresses close to her chest and hopelessly wrinkling the fabric. "Oh, the biscuits. A-*choo!*"

Cara returned her attention to the grounds outside her chambers. "It is a sorry life indeed if you find joy in biscuits and scones," she said, unable to keep the bitterness from her tone. Then really, what happiness was there? It assuredly was not found in the cold families a lord and lady were born into.

"Oh, but surely you see it is a lovely day?"

She squinted out into the dreary, gray-white, winter sky. A lovely day? Was the girl madder than a hatter? Her mistress had been summarily forgotten by her sole surviving parent at Christmas. Not that it mattered whether or not it was the holiday season. She abhorred all the false festive cheer of Christmas; a time when lords and ladies pretended they were happy and kind and all things different than the cold, unfeeling figures they truly were.

"I daresay it will be a wonderful holiday." Her maid wiped her nose on a handkerchief and quickly stuffed it into the front pocket sewn into her apron.

On what did the girl base such a surely erroneous assumption? What joyfulness did she know as a maid in the Duke of Ravenscourt's employ for Cara's miserable self?

"The skies are gray, without a hint of sunshine," she said, hating that she engaged the girl, but it provided a small distraction from her own miseries.

"Ah, but the smell of snow is in the air." Then, as though she could smell anything more than the dark, lonely chambers through her stuffed up nose, the girl threw her arms wide and inhaled deep. She ruined that attempt at invigoration with another sneeze.

A knock sounded at the door and Alison rushed over to open it. Cara thrust back her pathetic musings, despising the weak creature who still mourned the loss of a father's love, nearly as much as she despised the man himself. As Alison pulled the door open, one of Mrs. Belden's instructors—aptly named dragons—remained in the corridor. She whispered something to the maid. Cara pointedly kept her attention at the window, away from that slight exchange. All the while, her neck pricked with humiliated hurt at the obvious reason for the interruption.

Down the length of the gravel drive, a black carriage rattled toward the front of the establishment. Her heart gave a funny leap. With blossoming hope, she pressed her face to the window and squinted. Young ladies did not squint and they certainly did not show enthusiasm or, well, *any* hint of emotion. But she didn't give a jot about proper ladylike behavior just then. A cry, born of a hope she didn't believe herself capable of, stuck in her throat. For there was a carriage rattling slowly down the drive and that black conveyance signified she'd *not* been forgotten. She brushed a hand over the frosted pane, the glass ice cold on her bare palm. Ignoring the slight sting, she attended that elegant, black barouche as it came to a sudden stop outside the front of the revered finishing school.

An odd emptiness settled in her chest. She stared unblinkingly down at the crest—the crest of someone else's father. A sire who likely didn't love his daughter, because none of those self-important, officious peers who ruled the world did, but one who, at the very least, had not forgotten his daughter at the holiday times, either.

Alison cleared her throat. Schooling her features, Cara turned around. "What is it?" Her sharp tone came from a woman who was one word too many away from dissolving into a mewling, weepy mess.

The girl's usually sunny smile dipped. "Mrs. Belden asked to see you in her office, my lady."

She curled her hands into tight fists. *The summons.* Cara stole one more glance out the window and stared at the intersecting lines of her palm marked upon the frosted glass. Through that space left by her hand, the faint flecks of snow began to fall. *Prove me wrong. Come now. I command it.* From a place where she didn't know hope still dwelled within her, Cara willed another carriage down the drive. Except, just as she'd been a girl of seven willing her mother to breathe once more, no matter how long she stared or how much she wished it to be, it was not coming.

"My lady?"

It was that warm gentleness that snapped her from her miserable standstill. "Hurry along with the remainder of my belongings," she forced past tight lips. Cara spun on her heel and marched from the room, though it was remarkably hard to save face when you ordered your maid to pack your belongings and there was really no place to go.

Cara moved through the quiet, now empty, halls of this place that was no more home than the cold, empty halls of any one of her father's opulent estates. Mrs. Belden's, just like His Grace's townhouses and grand estates, was nothing more than a place with a roof and any number of walls and windows and doors. There was no warmth here.

Though, once upon a lifetime ago, there had been a place she'd considered home.

…but Father says you are to only call me Clarisse…

…ah, your father insisted you be named Clarisse, but I am your mama, and Cara mia, you shall always be…

Cara came to a sudden, staggering stop outside Mrs. Belden's office as the long-buried memory trickled in. She'd not allowed herself to think of her mother in the eleven years since she'd been gone. For with those thoughts came the aching reminder of what it had once meant to laugh and smile and be happy. She pressed her eyes closed and willed back all remembrances of the last person who'd loved her, not for what she could do or bring to someone else, but simply for herself.

"But I despise her."

That plaintive entreaty cut across Cara's thoughts and brought her eyes flying open. She stared at the wooden panel of Mrs. Belden's closed office door where the nasty headmistress now spoke to Lady Nora. Lady Nora Turner, the Earl of Derby's daughter, and one of Cara's greatest enemies at Mrs. Belden's. Though in truth, it was really more a tie for the top place among the ten other girls who'd had the misfortune of being scuttled off to Belden's lair.

"Everyone despises her," the woman spoke with a crisp matter-of-factness. She thumped her cane once. "But she is a duke's daughter and as such, is afforded our respect."

"I don't respect her," the fiery-spirited lady groused. "I hate her."

The muscles of Cara's stomach knotted at the blunt admission. Of course Nora hated her. They *all* hated her. From the students to servants here and in her father's home. She furrowed her brow. With the exception of the obstinate, always cheerful Alison. Cara flattened her lips into a hard line. Which was well and fine. She despised them all for their silly, joyful smiles and grating giggles and for their abundant reasons to be happy when she had none.

"Even so, do you expect your father would allow the Duke of Ravenscourt's daughter to be left here because you do not like her?"

"I did not say I do not like her. I said I hate her."

And if she didn't herself abhor the other young woman so much, she'd have admired her for going toe to toe with the vile dragon.

"She cannot very well stay here for the holiday."

"Why? *You* do." Desperation and confusion leant the girl's words a high pitch.

The headmistress sputtered. Young ladies did not challenge the woman.

A smile pulled Cara's lips; the feel of it rusty and painful from ill-use. Her grin withered at the other student's next words.

"I am sure her father will eventually remember he's forgotten her."

That was a wager Lady Nora would handily lose.

Another thump of the cane. "A duke does not forget his children." And that was another misspoken statement from this combative pair. The duke had forgotten more birthdays than Cara remembered. A memory slipped in.

"You are as pretty as a princess, Cara mia."

Mother placed her hands upon her shoulders and they stared at Cara's visage in the full-length mirror.

Cara cast an eager glance over her shoulder. *"Papa is truly taking me to Gunter's?"*

"Why, it is your birthday, dear."

The excited laughter trilled around the chambers of her mind.

She'd waited all day—and he'd never come.

Cara blinked. Where had the thirteen-year-old memory come from? For she'd been summarily forgotten at various points through her life.

This, however, was the first time she'd been so forgotten during the holidays. She blinked several times as a sheen misted her vision. Dratted dust. Odd, she'd never noticed the immaculate establishment was so dusty, and yet, how to account for this odd blurring? "A duke is very busy with matters far more pressing than his children."

To those powerful noblemen, *all* matters were more important than his children. With the exception of his heir, of course. She'd spent years hating Cedric for their father's favor. Then she'd spent the other years hating him for being as coolly indifferent as their sire.

"It will be a short carriage ride and then she will continue on to the duke's estates for Christmas. I consider this matter concluded, Lady Nora."

Blast and double blast. A carriage ride with Lady Nora, a girl who despised Cara and would delight in her misery? Perhaps being summarily forgotten and forced to dwell in the lair of the other dragons was preferable. She rapped once.

"Enter."

Cara pressed the handle and swept inside. Carrying her shoulders with a stately bearing even her father would have been forced to find pride in, she pulled the door closed and ran a cool, condescending look over Lady Nora. A flush stained the girl's cheeks and by the way she tightened her hands into balls at her sides, she was as prepared to resume the physical blows they'd come to six months earlier when Cara had single-handedly seen their instructor, Miss Jane Munroe, tossed out. Guilt knotted her belly.

"That will be all for now, Lady Nora," Mrs. Belden said in dismissal. She thumped her cane once in a manner more befitting a witch wielding the magic of her broom that would see the other girl vanish.

The two young ladies eyed each other a long moment. Cara met the vitriol and loathing teeming from the other lady's gaze with an icy derision. She'd not allow Nora the triumph of knowing her words and sneers had wounded like a well-placed barb.

"I said that will be all for now, Lady Nora," Mrs. Belden gave a tellingly furious two thumps of her cane.

As Lady Nora passed closely by Cara, the young woman yanked her skirts back.

The spectacle-wearing dragon spoke as soon as the door closed loudly behind the other student. "Your father failed to send 'round his carriage to collect you, my lady."

She'd known as much. The already eight departed carriages and the barren halls indicated all those slightly aware parents had sent for their daughters. While her own power-driven father, consumed by his own lofty status and advancing his wealth, could not be bothered to even send his servants to collect her. For Christmas. Having the headmistress utter those words aloud only made the truth of her circumstances all the more real.

Cara stood stiffly, silent as Mrs. Belden moved around her desk and claimed a seat at the head of the immaculate, broad, mahogany piece. She eyed her over the rims of her thick spectacles. "Most ladies would be in tears by such a fact, my lady." She eyed her with a pride better reserved for a mother to a daughter. "I am pleased with your absolute dignity and reserve in the face of your father's inactions this day."

It was an ill-testament to the person she'd become in her eighteen years that this headmistress, as hated as a venomous serpent, should find pride in her. "You summoned me, Mrs. Belden," Cara said with the ducal chill she'd heard in the handful of exchanges she'd had with her absentee father. "Say whatever else you'd say so we might," she dusted a speck of imagined dust from her puffed white sleeve, "conclude our business here."

The other woman froze a moment but then another one of those cold, dark smiles hinted at her pleasure. She no doubt applauded Cara's frigidity. "Will you please sit, my lady?"

She eyed the hard, wood chair at the foot of the desk, filled with a childlike urge to hurl that piece across this hated office, into the fire, and then take off running into the world outside, running as far and as fast as her legs could carry her, away from this world and into another where she ceased to be *this* and managed to be someone else—

"My lady?" Mrs. Belden eyed Cara standing there like she was an oddity on display at the Egyptian Center.

Except, after her mother's death, she'd spent her life being the perfect, ducal daughter and knew no other way. With wooden steps, she walked with a long-practiced calm over to the proffered chair and sat.

"Lady Nora is to leave today. She has graciously agreed to allow you to accompany her. From there you will then be given leave of the earl's carriage to return to His Grace for the holiday." For the holiday. That last part may as well have been nothing more than an afterthought. Holidays were not celebrated in the Duke of Ravenscourt's home. As they did not advance his power or prestige, he'd never allowed those festivities and inane affairs. All they were, anyway, were artificial moments of false happiness.

The leader of the dragons steepled her fingers and rested them on her desk. She stared at Cara, expecting, what? Thanks for being shuffled off, humiliated and shamed, in Lady Nora's carriage? A promise to speak favorably to the powerful Duke of Ravenscourt? Alas, the woman still did not realize the duke preferred his hounds and horses to his one daughter.

Cara spoke and when she did, she stripped all emotion, all hint of caring, and even the disdain she felt for one who'd bow before an almighty duke for his total alone. "Is there anything else you wish to speak with me about, Mrs. Belden? I would oversee my maid's packing of my belongings." It was a blatant lie. By now, Alison had likely already clicked the trunk closed.

Mrs. Belden frowned. "That is all." She pursed her lips, likely in an attempt to keep from saying more.

With a toss of her head, Cara rose with the graceful care ingrained into her by the army of nursemaids and governesses who'd reared her and swept from the room.

CARA SAT RIGID ON THE seat of the Earl of Derby's carriage, alongside her sniffling maid. Her body carefully angled as it was, and had been for the better part of the journey, had developed an ache that traveled from her neck, down her shoulders, and to her hips. The same stilted silence that had fallen the moment Lady Nora's groom had closed the carriage door at Mrs. Belden's Finishing School had stretched on for these two hours.

The seventeen-year-old lady with her outspoken thoughts on anything and everything from a woman's place in the world to Cara's constant frown, as she called it, broke the silent impasse. "I did not want to bring you."

Alison burrowed against the wall of the carriage, as though she were trying to escape the charged exchange.

Cara bit the inside of her cheek. It should not matter that this surly, deservedly angry lady abhorred her, and yet, strangely, an odd pang struck her chest. Refusing to give the other young woman any idea that her words had any effect, she flicked a cool gaze over her frame. "I do not care whether you wished to bring me or not." Then, in a bid to ruffle the infuriatingly cool woman she peeled her lip back. "Furthermore, you've already indicated as much, two," four, "times now. Your words grow tedious."

Lady Nora narrowed her gaze and Cara stiffened. That harsh glint in the lady's eyes matched the fury right before she'd backhanded Cara across the mouth for having told one of the instructors about the scandalous material being taught by former instructor Mrs. Jane Munroe. "I do not like you, Clarisse Falcot."

That was rather disappointing. With the lady's inventive curses and harsh words, she was capable of far more originality than "I do not like you". In fact, if she truly wished a rise out of Cara, a more astounding revelation would have been if the girl stated her regard. "I have not liked you for your smug, condescending looks since I entered the school. And I have hated you since your actions resulted in Mrs. Munroe's firing."

The pebble of guilt grew to a large stone in Cara's belly. Mrs.

Munroe. Cara's father's illegitimate daughter-turned-instructor at Mrs. Belden's. There had been whispers amongst the instructors which had fueled whispers amongst the students and then the tittering comments and loud whispers had ensued about a duke who cared for his illegitimate child more than his rightfully born one. Which in retrospect was utter rubbish. Her father didn't care about anyone. She curled her toes into the soles of her serviceable boots. Of all the detestable acts she was guilty of in her life, getting her half-sister sacked had been the greatest offense. What kind of black, ugly soul did she possess that she could so impulsively ruin another woman's life, without considering the ramifications until it was too late?

"You, of course, have nothing to say," Lady Nora seethed. "You sit there in all your pompous glory as though you are yourself the Duke of Ravenscourt or a member of the Queen's Court, but the truth is you are nothing, Clarisse Falcot. You are nothing more than an unwanted daughter, whose father cannot even bring himself to remember at Christmas and who will go on to be a leading Society matron and produce equally unkind and cold offspring. I pity the gentleman who will be tied to you."

Cara searched around inside for the deserved fury and the biting scorn for the young woman's venomous tirade. And yet, for some reason, she could not force out the proper words past this blasted lump in her throat. Instead, she pasted on a practiced, hardened grin. With slow, precise movements, she presented her back once more. Aware of the young woman studying her for some sign of weakness or emotion and any other reaction Cara was determined to deny her, she pulled aside the red velvet curtain.

She damned the faint tremble to her fingertips and blamed it on the winter cold. Snow and ice hit noisily off the lead windows and she stared out at those pure white specks as they swirled and danced in the air. Lord Derby's horses trudged ahead at a slow, steady clip through the snow-covered countryside. The two young ladies continued the remaining trek in stilted silence.

And as they neared the end of their journey to the Earl of Derby's property, Cara came to the sad, staggering truth that she far preferred the idea of remaining with the unkind Lady Nora to returning to face the father who'd forgotten her.

"At last," the other woman muttered.

Cara drew back the curtain once more as Lady Nora's home pulled into focus. Though sprawling, the country estate would be considered modest compared to her father's ducal holdings. And yet, she'd happily trade her own empty home for a father who did not forget her. Cara bit the inside of her cheek hard. No, that wasn't altogether true. She'd trade it all for a father who cared. For *someone* who cared. Then, what person would care about someone who'd become such a hollow shell of a human being that she no longer knew how to show or feel any emotion outside of bitterness? Her throat worked spasmodically.

The carriage drew to a halt and she gave her head a clearing shake, in a bid to dislodge her maudlin sentiments. The conveyance dipped as the groom scrambled from his perch. Moments later, the liveried servant opened the door. "Lady Nora," the man greeted with a smile and reached inside.

"Thomasly," she returned with a cheerful grin Cara had not believed the other woman capable of. Then, perhaps it was merely her for whom she reserved her vitriol.

From within the confines of the carriage, she studied the exchange between servant and lady. The two chatted more than Cara's maid about her morning meals. Surely the earl did not allow such familiarities between his daughter and his staff, particularly the male members of his household?

A memory slipped in of the days following her mother's passing, of Cara's visits to the stables. The scent of horseflesh and hay still as sharp in her mind now as it had been those eleven years ago. For the agony of losing her mother, she found solace in the stables alongside the grooms. Those coarse and gruff servants who showed her the proper way to brush a horse… Until her father had stormed in and, with his hand clamped about her arm, forcefully led her back to the house. It was the last time she'd ever visited that dark, comforting place.

Cara blinked. She'd not remembered that moment—until now.

She dimly registered the stares of Lady Nora and the groom fixed on her and gave a quick shake of her head.

"Well, come along," Lady Nora snapped.

Schooling her features into the hardened, practiced mask she donned for anyone and everyone, Cara held her hand out and allowed the once smiling, now stoic, groom to help her down. The other young woman moved at an almost sprint up the steps, while Cara followed at a more sedate pace that came from years of lady-like decorum being drilled into her—as well as a desire to have as much distance between herself and this lady who so disliked her.

As though the entire household had been in waiting for this very moment, the front doors were thrown open and a butler greeted Lady Nora with a beaming smile. All the while, Cara picked her way up the steps, trying to escape notice, a rather impossible feat considering she'd imposed upon the charity of the earl's daughter, and still the favor was not complete.

A cry went up and Cara jumped, slapping a hand to her errati-cally beating heart. And then, she froze at the threshold. A towering, broad, bear of a man swallowed Lady Nora in a hug while a deli-cate, thin slip of a woman stood with her fingertips to her lips. By the deep brown hue of the older woman's eyes and the slight cleft in the man's chin, the couple before her was none other than Lady Nora's parents.

A swell of envy so potent and powerful filled Cara's chest. She gripped the edge of the doorway a moment to keep the world from swaying. For the misery she'd known as the forgotten daugh-ter of the Duke of Ravenscourt, there had been solace in knowing that all those self-important noblemen treated their female off-spring thusly. This intimate moment between mother, father, and daughter, however, proved an altogether different tale. She cast a look over her shoulder into the increasing storm. For their tale made her long for the biting cold of the snow outside to this wholly special moment exchanged between father and daughter.

"Papa, this is Lady Clarisse Falcot."

Cara stiffened as the butler hurried to close the door behind her and the earl and countess shifted their attention to their unex-pected and unwanted guest.

Broad, where her own father was lean and wiry, the earl sketched a deep bow. "My lady," he said with the cool reserve bestowed a duke's daughter.

She preferred the unrestrained loving father he'd been mere moments ago. Cara inclined her head at a lofty angle and dropped a deep curtsy. "My lord. Thank you for the use of your carriage." How did her words not shake with the hurt and embarrassment still running through her?

"The duke forgot her," Lady Nora said by way of explanation.

Mother and Father turned matching glowers on their cherished daughter.

She wrinkled her nose. "He did." The spirited miss looked to Cara with a bold insolence that only deepened her mother's frown. "And with good reason. She is horrid."

"Nora," the countess scolded. A gracious and flawless hostess, the older woman came forward with her hands extended. "We are honored you will be spending the holiday season with us."

From beyond her mother's shoulder, Nora choked. "The hol—"

Cara snapped her damp, emerald green, muslin cloak, smattering the marble foyer with bits of melted snow. "I thank you for the gracious offer. However, I truly must leave now. My fath—" The lie died a quick death.

"Now?" The earl furrowed his high, noble brow. "The storm is worsening."

"Which is why it is imperative I leave posthaste. If you'd be so gracious as to allow me the use of your carriage." So that she could slink off, the shamed, laughed about, unloved duke's daughter, while retaining some level of pride.

"But—"

"My family is expecting me," she said in clipped tones when the earl made to protest once more. This time she fed him the lie they all knew to be a lie. Life had taught her that people did not challenge a duke's kin. She wrinkled her nose. Well, Lady Nora did. And a handful of the other distinguished students at Mrs. Belden's. But never before their parents.

This moment proved that truth.

"Of course," the earl said. "I will see the team of horses switched."

Standing in the foyer of this bucolic family, Cara huddled deep into the fabric of her damp cloak. What an odd place to be; not wanting to stay with this happy, loving lot, but not wanting to board the earl's carriage and return to her own life, either...

And in this moment, being honest with at least herself, Cara indulged the wish she had in her heart this Christmas—to be loved for nothing but herself.

CHAPTER 3

ALISON WAS NOT SMILING. OR prattling. Her flushed cheeks and feverish eyes killed all evidence of her habitual mirth. The absolute silence of Cara's maid was only further heightened by the wind howling outside the Earl of Derby's carriage. This was very dire, indeed.

Cara drew the curtain back and peered out into the thick swirl of snowflakes. Then the conveyance stopped. "Why has the carriage stopped?" Did those words belong to her or Alison? A niggling of unease pitted in her belly.

"I am sure we are merely stopping for a moment because…" Her maid eyed her skeptically. "Because…" Well, blast what was there to stop for in this desolate landscape painted white? "Highwaymen?" Alison breathed, fear dripping from that one word. "*A-choo!*"

The girl's tendency for the dramatics eased some of Cara's attention and she gave a roll of her eyes. "Highwaymen do not traverse this road." It was too well-traveled. She caught her lower lip between her teeth. At least, she didn't *think* they did. Schooling her features into an expressionless mask, she peeked through the crack in the velvet curtains and squinted out into the rapidly falling snow. The muscles of her stomach clenched. What if her overly imaginative maid proved correct and there was a blasted highwayman? Wouldn't that just prove her rotted luck this day?

She tensed her jaw. They could make off with every last one of her possessions, but there was one that would have to be pried from her fingers.

"Do you see them?" Did the clattering of the girl's teeth have to do with her fever or the cold?

They both jumped as someone banged on the carriage door. Cara's heart climbed into her throat and she studiously avoided Alison's I-told-you-there-would-be-highwaymen looks. With trembling fingers, she peeled open the curtain and brushed her gloved hand over the iced pane. Some of the tension went out of her. The earl's groom tugged his cap lower and made to knock once more.

Cara pushed it open. A blast of snow slapped at her face and the cold of it momentarily sucked her breath away. "What—?" The winter wind stole all sound from her words.

The groom cupped his hands about his mouth. "The carriage is stuck, my lady."

She tipped her head. "Stuck?"

He nodded once. "We passed an inn a short while back, but we will have to walk the remainder of the way. The drifts are too high on the roads."

Her heart sank into her stomach. "Walk?" She knew she must sound something of a lackwit repeating back every other one of the servant's words, and yet—"Are you mad?" she shouted into the wind. By God, they would perish in this Godforsaken storm.

"It is not far," he called back and then held out a hand.

A spark of fear lit Alison's glassy eyes, but she accepted the groom's hand and allowed him to assist her down. The maid's serviceable boots disappeared into the thick snow and her lips parted on a gasp as she tugged her cloak closer.

Cara's thoughts raced as she took in the couple shivering outside the carriage. "But surely—?"

"The carriage cannot be moved," he said impatiently.

On its own volition, her gaze swung to the roof of the black barouche to where her trunk sat atop—and her mother's necklace. Now she would pay the price for her own foolish pride. "But my belongings?" Panic raised the tone of her words to a high pitch. She could not leave her trunk. Not when the last piece belonging to her mother rested within its confines.

"I will have to return for it." She would have to be stone deaf to fail to hear the impatience in the older servant's tone.

Cara reached for her bonnet and set it atop her head, deftly tying the long, velvet ribbons underneath. Words of protest hovered on her lips.

…you will not so shame yourself by showing that you care about anything or anyone, Clarisse Victoria Falcot…

Her gut churned at the long-forgotten words drawled by her father from across his office desk. "Very well," she said with a regality even her father would have a difficult time faulting and accepted the servant's hand. Her boots sank deep into the snow, wringing a shocked gasp from her as her ankles disappeared into the drift. "Bloody hell." And if she weren't so blasted cold she'd have felt some heat of embarrassment at her scandalous utterance.

The groom's lips twitched as he turned his efforts to unhitching the horses. A short while later, he motioned Cara and Alison to follow. Her Falcot pride had gotten her into this bumble broth. She forcibly lifted her legs and snow-dampened hem, struggling to maintain her balance as they walked slowly back to an inn she'd not even seen in their travels.

At her side, Alison gave a piteous moan. "We are going to die out here." Now the girl would choose to abandon her sunny disposition?

"I am not going to die out here," she mumbled to herself. She was too bloody enraged about the whole blasted day. She focused on that rage to keep from thinking about how the wind slapped painfully at her cheeks, stinging her eyes with snow. With each step she took, she fed that fury. Forgotten by her father. One step. Forgotten also by her brother, if one wanted to be truly precise in their upset. Another step. Forgotten at Christmas. Yet another step. She cupped her hands around her mouth. "Where is this blasted inn?" she shouted.

The servant jabbed his finger ahead, not breaking stride. And for one horrifying moment, she believed this had all been a deliberate ploy by her enemy Lady Nora, and the girl had somehow convinced the loyal, smiling-for-his-mistress groom to abandon Cara and her maid here in the middle of the wild, in the midst of a storm.

Pride was a dangerous thing. Trudging through the snow, with her cloak little protection from the harsh elements beating down on her face and cutting through her clothes, Cara readily conceded there were reasons for all those lessons, proverbs and statements about the blasted vice. Her teeth chattered, the sound of it swallowed by the howling winter wind and then, through the thick curtain of snow rapidly falling, a small establishment pulled into focus. "Thank God," she breathed, stirring puffs of air with her breath.

They trudged the remainder of the way to the stables outside the inn. The earl's groom rapped loudly on the wood doors which were thrown open by an old, graying man. He eyed them a moment. Whatever words were exchanged between the two were lost to the howling wind. Moments later, they marched up to the front of the old inn. The groom pushed the door open. Shivering inside her hopelessly damp cloak, she looked about the dark establishment. A thick haze of smoke filled the taproom from a recently lit pipe. The pungent scent burned her lungs. Cara wrinkled her nose. She'd always detested the nauseating smell. It was a scent that drew forth memories of her father closeted away in his billiards room while he entertained other pompous noblemen who were all vastly more important than his own daughter.

A weak Alison hovered at her shoulder, eying the empty taproom.

Cara tugged off her wet gloves and continued to pass her gaze over the dimly lit space, searching for the owner of that foul cheroot. A fire raged in the hearth, casting eerie shadows about the cracked and chipped walls. "Hello?" she called out in an icy tone. From the back of the establishment, footsteps shuffled.

A portly, white-haired man with a pipe stuck between his teeth, rushed forward to greet them. "Ah, in need of rooms are you?"

Did he think she preferred to spend her night out of doors in this violent storm? Cara bit back the tart response. "I require a room," she said tightly, dusting her gloves together. She cast a glance at Alison. "That is, two rooms." After all, it wouldn't do to be *quite* so alone in the miserable inn.

The innkeeper removed his pipe and grinned, displaying a row of cracked and missing teeth. She rocked back on her heels, nearly bowled over by the scent of stale garlic on his breath.

"And meals," she said.

At her side, Alison sneezed into her elbow.

"And a warm bath."

The older innkeeper took another puff of his pipe. "Is there anything else, my lady?"

She gave a brusque shake of her head, and shrugged out of her dampened cloak, and turned it over to the older man's care. "That is all."

An equally wizened woman with shocking white hair and a twinkle in her rheumy eyes rushed forward. "Allow me to show you to your rooms, my lady."

Cara held up a staying hand and cast a look back at the earl's driver. "I would have my trunk brought abovestairs immediately."

The man opened his mouth, but a large gust of wind slammed into the door, rattling it on its frame and beating against the lead windowpanes. He doffed his hat and beat the wet piece against his leg. "But my lady, the storm…"

Her heart started and she turned her attention to the window. Why in blazes had she not carried her heart pendant on her person? *Because you were so hurt and angry at your father's inactions this day, that you spitefully lashed out at the piece given you by the one person who ever loved you.* Her throat worked painfully. And what had she done? Had her maid bury it into the bottom of her cold trunk. *This bloody day.* Nay. It was her blasted impulsivity. Jane Munroe slid into her thoughts once more and Cara forcefully thrust the kind, former instructor's visage from her mind.

Cara squinted out into the dark as a blanket of white snow swirled past the frosted pane. She swung back to face the driver and set her jaw to hide the faint quake there. "I require my belongings this instant." The gowns and other fripperies she'd been granted as the daughter of a duke could go hang. Her heart pounded with panic. "I need—" *My mother's necklace.* The assembled collection of servants fixed peculiar looks on her. Cara's skin went hot. "Dry clothing," she finished lamely. "I require dry clothing."

The old woman beamed. "Well, that is easy enough, my lady. I've several lovely gowns. Nowhere near the fancy garments you are accustomed to." She turned to go.

"No," Cara cried out and her utterance echoed around the inn, earning shocked silence. She turned back to the earl's driver and forced her tone into a semblance of icy calm "Go."

The earl's servant shifted on his feet with the gusting storm raging its fury at the door. "But, my lady," he whispered. "It is *snowing*."

She took a step toward him. "It is a bit of snow and I command you to go." *Please go.*

He dropped his unrepentant stare to her wet boots.

"You'd send a person out into this Godforsaken weather for your own fripperies, brat?"

A harsh, angry voice sounded beyond her shoulder and she spun about. Her heart stilled and fear settled like a stone in her belly at the big, broad, bear of a man glowering down at her. She fisted the fabric of her gown and swallowed hard. A man who glowered at her. With the gruff stubble on his face and towering height, the imposing stranger wore the rank of his lesser class like a stamp upon his skin. As though he'd followed the direction her thoughts had traveled, he narrowed his blue, nearly black eyes in a menacing fashion. She swallowed hard and backed away from him.

A mocking grin pulled at his hard lips. "Nothing to say, brat?"

Outrage blotted out the nervousness swirling in her belly. Brat? Why, the lout had called her brat. Twice. And challenged her, before this small, shocked cluster of strangers. Finding her courage, she settled her feet on the wood floor. "How dare you?" She prided herself on those evenly delivered words when inside she quaked. By God, the man was a foot taller than her own five-foot four-inch frame and his powerful muscles strained the confines of his coarse garments.

He folded his arms at his chest, stretching the fabric of his white sleeves over his defined biceps. She really had no place ogling a figure such as him and yet—she warmed. She'd spent most of her life filing men into the category of worthless, shiftless bounders such as her father. Never before had she admired a man, and warmed at his mere presence, alone.

"How dare I? You are a spoiled ice princess who'd send out her servants to rescue what? Your fine gowns?" His condescending opinion jerked her back from her foolhardy musings with all the effect of being dumped into that icy snow outside.

Cara ground her teeth. "Do *not* call me ice princess. Furthermore," she raked a gaze over him. "It is not your business." What should she expect a rude-mannered lout such as this one to understand about that necklace buried in the bottom of her trunk?

He took another step closer and her courage deserted her. "Not my business?"

Oh, dear. She'd never before been expected to account for her opinions to anyone beyond her father. And he cared even less for her opinions than he did for her on the whole. Cara retreated until her back collided with the wooden door. She winced, managing a jerky nod. "That is correct. N-not your business."

"Not my business that a spoiled lady would send a man out into a bloody blizzard for her fancy baubles?" A seething fury graveled his voice.

His highhandedness grated on her last nerve. In a bid to goad him, she tipped her chin up a notch. "I see by your words, you at least understand." What did he know anything of her?

It proved the wrong thing to say. He ate away the distance between them in three long strides. His alacrity wrung a gasp from her and she held her hands up to ward him off, but he continued coming until a hairsbreadth separated them.

Even weakened from fever, Alison managed a fierce look for the stranger. "How dare you? Do you know who—?"

Cara glanced around the hulking beast's shoulder, silencing the girl. It would hardly do to reveal the truth of her birthright before this thunderous brute. Despite his cultured tones, he clearly detested those of noble birthrights. He was likely some indulgent nobleman's by-blow son who despised anyone and everyone of the peerage. Who knew what an uncouth lout such as he would do with the truth of her identity?

"I do not give a jot if your mistress is the Queen of England," he directed his icy words to Cara. He stuck a finger under her nose and she went cross-eyed staring down at it. "If you are in such desperate need of your fineries, then risk your own life but not another person's."

She wanted to spew rancorous words at him, lauding her station and birthright that would effectively silence him. Except, by the unrelenting set of his strong, square jaw, this man would never be suitably, or even unsuitably, impressed by any of that. Cara swatted his hand. "You mannerless lout. Do not put your finger near my face."

"Mannerless I may be, but I am not a self-centered snob who'd put my own well-being before that of another's because of some inflated sense of self-worth."

That harsh accusation ran through her. Never before had anyone spoken to her so. There was something humbling in being so disparaged by a person's words and his thoughts. Only, this desperation was not for her fineries and fripperies as he'd called them, but rather for one *particular* finery. "You know nothing about it," she bit out between clenched teeth.

"Oh, don't I?"

"No, you don't!"

The servants swung their heads back and forth, as though they took in a game of racquets.

A wry, condescending smile pulled harder at his hard lips. "Nor do I care to know anything about it."

It, as in *her*. Humiliation slapped her cheeks with heat. Embarrassment…but something more blended with that emotion. Hurt. Which made little sense, and surely could only be accounted for by her blasted maudlin thoughts at this silly time of the season with her father's latest display of indifference.

The earl's driver cleared his throat. "I-I can fetch my lady's belongings."

She swallowed back bitter regret. A bit late for that. All of this mortifying exchange could have been avoided if he'd made that *offer* before this uncouth stranger put his aquiline nose in her affairs. Cara gave a brusque nod and the man turned to go.

"You will do no such thing." The brute's icy, commanding tone would have impressed her austere duke of a father.

Pain stabbed at her heart. In a desperate bid to feign nonchalance, Cara snapped her skirts, and with her nose in the air, stepped around the servant's champion. "I would like to be shown to my rooms." That request contained what little remained of her pride.

"Of course." The old woman rushed over. "If you'll follow me." She motioned to Cara and Alison.

With her neck burning from the hard gaze the stranger fixed on her, she forced her steps into the practiced, unhurried ones meant to convey control when all she wanted to do was shut herself away in the miserable rooms of this inn, lock the door, curl up in a heap on her borrowed bed, and forget this whole blasted day.

CHAPTER 4

Seated alongside the blazing fire in the empty taproom, William stared into the contents of his tankard. His earlier peace and calm had been effectively stolen by a tart-mouthed, self-important lady. He scowled and then took another swig of his drink.

All the golden-tressed harridan had done was rouse thoughts of the pretentious lady his parents would see him wed to; one of those young ladies who put her own material desires before the safety and security of a servant, or anyone, as long as her needs were met.

It really was quite a shame that a lean, lithe creature with the heart-shaped face of an angel and that pale blonde hair should be as frigid as a January freeze. He'd like to kiss the frown from the lush contours of her lips and melt that icy veneer. He growled. He'd been too long without a bloody woman if he was lusting after that one.

The innkeeper shuffled over and motioned to William's drink. "Another?"

William gave thanks for the timely interruption from the fleeting madness of lusting after the ice princess. He smiled and held his nearly empty glass out to be refilled. "Fine ale, thank you…?" He stared expectantly up at the older man.

"Martin. My name is Martin and my wife is Martha," he motioned to the old woman running a rag over empty tables.

He lifted his tankard in salute. "Fine ale," he lied. It was blasted rubbish stuff.

A twinkle lit Martin's eyes. "Kind of you to say as much." He dropped his voice to a conspiratorial whisper. "But it is lousy stuff." He nodded off to his wife and William followed his stare. "But I do not have the heart to tell her that it's as bad as our accommodations here." He waggled his eyebrows. "Takes pride in this place and I'm content to let her believe we run the finest inn in the king's kingdom." Martin gave a wink. "Then, that is what you do when you're in love, isn't it?"

His smile grew brittle. To conceal that telling gesture, he took a sip of his awful ale. "Indeed," he murmured. He'd never personally experienced that sentiment and with the future his parents expected of him, he never would. The man made to move, but William motioned to the seat opposite him. "Please, sit." On a cold, dreary night like this, he didn't welcome being alone with thoughts of the life awaiting him. The old innkeeper swiftly set down his jug and claimed the rickety chair William had indicated.

In actuality, William knew nothing of being in love. His own parents' marriage was a happy union, so he did not doubt that reality existed for *some* gentlemen. It just would not be him. For even as this man and that nameless harpie abovestairs who believed him to be a coarse commoner with his pockets to let…the truth was, he'd someday ascend to the vaunted title of duke. As such, those simple, but important pleasures afforded others—the ability to bind them to a person they respected and admired, and mayhap even loved— well, that was not a luxury afforded all members of the *ton*.

The servant cut into the silence. "Do you have a lady you call wife?" he asked, following the path William's thoughts had wandered.

"No wife." Not yet. He took another sip, welcoming the warmth afforded him by the miserable contents of his drink. But there would be. God help him, there would be. His throat burned for the sting of more drink and he raised his glass once more.

"Ah, the lady abovestairs is indeed a lovely one."

William paused with his glass halfway to his lips. Surely he'd heard the man wrong. Or mayhap there was another, sweeter, smiling creature he'd not had the pleasure of meeting. He managed a noncommittal grunt.

That glimmer deepened in the man's eyes. "A spirited one, she is."

He rolled his shoulders. "She is a lady." And more specifically, the manner of cold, unfeeling figures he'd spent his life avoiding. It was enough that his parents would see him honor a connection to one of those very ladies. William clenched his jaw as the age-old resentment swirled through him. Nay, they could not have selected a woman who was, at the very least, pleasing and kind. His mother's devotion to her late friend had come before even William's own happiness.

Martin leaned close. "Eh, but then even with your coarse garments and bullish figure, I'm not supposed to believe you are anything other than a gentleman." He gave a wink.

William started. Craving the obscurity that came with being a titleless figure, he'd foolishly hoped those in this inn would fail to see past his unassuming attire.

"Your secret is yours, my lord," Martin assured.

He passed his drink back and forth between his hands. "Thank you." As it was, the freedoms enjoyed by him these years were nearing an end.

"She was a bit cold." Martin withdrew a stained kerchief and dabbed his brow. "But then, all ladies are a bit cold, and there is something to be said for those spirited creatures."

"Is there?" He infused a droll edge that earned a chuckle from the other man.

"Oh, of course. In your youth, you just don't realize it." He nodded toward his wife who'd moved on to cleaning another table. "My Martha is a spirited one. In her earlier days, she could out bellow the gruffest of men to enter these doors."

"There is a difference between spirited and unkind," William felt inclined to point out. And there was nothing redeeming in a woman who'd send her servant out into this fierce blizzard.

"Perhaps." Martin rocked back on the legs of his chair and hooked his fingers into the top of his pants. "But I always think there is more to a person than what is first seen upon the surface."

He bit back the retort. He'd not disabuse the innkeeper of his more hopeful thoughts. In actuality, William belonged to a world of cold, condescending nobles and had relished every moment of freedom from that same glittering society. His parents and siblings had proven the exception rather than the proverbial rule where the peerage was concerned.

"Martin, come along. The guests abovestairs require their meals."

The innkeeper settled his chair back upon the spindly legs and climbed to his feet with a sigh.

William touched the bridge of his imagined hat. "Good evening to you, Martin."

"My—"

"William," he cut in. "Just William." For he'd embrace this last strand of obscurity afforded him before he was thrust back into the world he'd spent years running from. As the man hurried off, a twinge of sympathy pulled at him. He did not envy the innkeeper his dealings with that shrew abovestairs.

CARA WALKED IN A CIRCLE, surveying her rooms. She rubbed her hands back and forth over her arms to drive back the chill that still lingered from her trek through the snow. Her efforts proved futile. With her sharp gaze, she took in everything from the cracked wash basin and pitcher to the scratched and scraped hardwood floor. She surveyed the thin, threadbare carpet at the foot of a too-lumpy bed. Perhaps it was not as uncomfortable as it appeared. Cara crossed over and sat on the bed. She placed her hands on the edge and shifted back and forth, testing the lumpy mattress. With a beleaguered sigh, she closed her eyes a moment and then in a move that would have earned a stiff recrimination from her father, flung her arms out and sprawled backward, with her head hanging off the edge of the bed. She glowered up at the cracked plaster ceiling with water marks hinting at wear to the roof.

Drip. Drip. Drip.

In the dimly lit space, she sought out that grating fall of water. A cold, wet drop landed on her nose. She followed the path up to the ceiling where a puddle of moisture pooled on the peeling paint. Cara slid her eyes closed. With the disastrous course of her day, why should she expect anything else? Another drop landed on her forehead and she rolled onto her side, disabusing the fates of the further pleasure of tormenting her.

Her teeth chattered noisily in the quiet space, punctuated by the gusting wind beating against the window. She drew her legs close to her chest and huddled in a ball and, because it was far easier to focus on a stranger who despised her than a father who did not care, she ran through her meeting with that brute in the taproom. His antipathy had been palpable and really should not matter. After all, no one liked her. And on most days, she did not even like herself. And yet… A blasted sheen of tears blurred her vision and she blinked them back.

Foolish signs of weakness, gel. Her father's thunderous admonishment echoed off these foreign walls.

She shivered and burrowed into the thin coverlet adorning her bed. "M-material p-possessions. Brat, you'll call me." Cara shifted and turned deeper into the blanket, futilely seeking warmth. "But you are w-wearing your w-warm garments and drinking your ale in front of the fire." And she would have traded all that material comfort as the lout had called it for that cherished gift left by her mother.

A knock sounded at the door and she surged to her feet. For a brief instant, she hung onto the hope the earl's driver had braved the beast's command and the winter storm to retrieve her trunk.

"My lady, I've brought you some things."

Her heart fell. Cara quickly dashed her hands over her eyes and then pinched her cheeks.

"My lady?"

She swung her legs over the edge of the bed and settled her feet on the floor. Then, hurrying across the room, she reached the wood panel and pulled it open just as the woman would have knocked again.

The white-haired woman froze with her hand poised to rap. A hesitant smile formed on her lips. "Oh, hello." She shifted the burden in her arms.

Cara's gaze went to the neatly folded garments held close to the innkeeper's chest. Though not the satins and silks her father insisted she be adorned in, the vibrancy of the emerald green fabric momentarily stole her thoughts from her misery.

Without asking to be admitted, the woman entered. "It is not the gowns you are surely accustomed to wearing, but still pretty nonetheless," she said with the same sunny disposition demonstrated by Alison.

She caught her lower lip as the woman laid the shift and under-garments upon the bed. As she prattled on, she snapped the dress open. The wrinkled muslin bore the evidence of its age in the pattern alone, and yet… "It is lovely," she said grudgingly.

The other woman widened her smile. A twinkle lit her eyes. "May I help you change?"

"My maid—"

"Is quite ill." She made a tsking sound. "The young girl has a fever and is quite chilled."

And now Alison was ill, which left Cara absolutely and totally alone in this dratted situation. Letting loose another sigh, she presented her back and allowed the woman to assist her with the bothersome row of buttons down the length of her white satin dress. The garment sailed down to her feet. She stepped out of it.

"I have prepared a holiday meal," the woman chatted happily as she drew Cara's shift overhead and reached for another aged, but blessedly dry, one.

What precisely was a holiday meal? She bit the inside of her cheek to keep from freeing that curious inquiry and stuck her arms into the presented arm holes.

"And now the dress." The woman pulled the muslin piece over Cara's head and set to work on the row of buttons along the back. "There." She eyed her handiwork a moment.

A cold drop fell on her hand and she followed it up to a new patch of dampened ceiling.

"Oh, dear," the woman murmured wringing her hands. "I dare-say this storm has not proven helpful to the ceiling."

And Cara would wager the current snow had little to do with the condition of her rooms and everything to do with years of neglect. She opened her mouth to say as much when that brutish stranger's earlier charges came rushing to the surface. By God she'd not feed that ill-opinion he'd drawn of her. She promptly pressed her lips into a tight line.

"Perhaps you might prefer to take your meal downstairs."

"Splendid idea," Cara muttered.

And preferring the beast downstairs to the cold, wet conditions of her dreary rented rooms, she followed after the woman who led her to a table already set with a plate. The innkeeper had been optimistic. She wrinkled her nose. Then, considering the rapid drip above that lumpy bed, she'd likely wagered no person, lord, lady, or lad on the streets would want to remain in *those* chambers.

"Here we are," the woman said. Her husband rushed over and pulled out the wooden chair. It wobbled on uneven legs. Cara hesitated beside the table and warily eyed the suspicious burnt portions on her plate. On stiff legs, she claimed the seat and gave the couple a dismissive nod.

The couple gone, Cara grimaced and picked up her fork. She shoved her fork around the holiday fare that might or might not have been some form of pudding. She picked some up on the edge of her utensil and carried it close to her eyes. If this was holiday food, then she most assuredly saw why Cook avoided these items on the menu.

Splat.

Cara wrinkled her nose as the ivory colored slop landed noisily amidst the burnt potatoes.

"Never tell me," a droll voice sounded beyond her shoulder, "you find yourself disapproving of your evening meal."

At that slightly mocking, rough baritone, she stiffened. "Surely you have something preferable to do this evening than to keep company with a brat," she gritted out, not taking her gaze from her plate.

With the effrontery better afforded a duke, he came around the table, pulled out the chair opposite her, and claimed the seat. His broad body filled the small, oak frame of the dining table. When no response was immediately forthcoming, she lifted her gaze, and found a sardonic half-grin on his lips. "Never tell me, I hurt your feelings, princess?"

She thinks she's a princess. And boys will want to marry her, but the only reason anyone will want her is because she's a duke's daughter.

That memory of her first day at Mrs. Belden's came rushing back and she stared unblinkingly at the opening of the stranger's white shirt. She'd not thought of that moment in years, so much so that she'd convinced herself that those ugly sniggerings hadn't really mattered. Why, with this man looking on, did she acknowledge the truth—it had mattered, mattered because they'd seen the lonely girl without a friend in the world as icy and aloof?

He passed his blue-black gaze searchingly over her face. "Where are your biting words, princess?" He tried to bait her. As one who'd fielded snide looks and cruel whispers, she recognized as much. Would he even care that his words had caused this tightening in her chest?

Heat burned her cheeks and she quickly dropped her gaze. "I have told you once, do not call me princess."

The legs of his chair scraped along the floor as he pulled closer to the table. "Never tell me I offended you…*princess?*"

Cara swallowed the scathing retort. Over the years she'd had far more formidable foes than him. She'd not let him needle her. Schooling her face into an expressionless mask, she winged an eyebrow upward. "You might call me a brat and self-important and all other manner of insults you've leveled at me, but I am not a bully." *Liar. You have been a bully plenty of times in the past.* Her half-sister, Jane's visage slipped to her mind and an odd pressure squeezed her heart—remorse. Through her impulsivity and a futile attempt to protect herself from the hurt of her father's disdain, she'd been the worst sort of bully to Jane Munroe. To rid her throat of the blasted lump there, Cara took a sip of the tepid glass of watered wine.

The stranger dropped his chestnut eyebrows. She braced for his taunting challenge. Instead, a frown played about his lips and he set his tankard on the table. "My apologies," he said quietly.

Cara yanked her startled gaze up to his. Men did not apologize. Not her domineering father, or her self-important brother, and certainly not rude strangers who challenged her in a taproom before servants. Nor was she deserving of that.

Another one of those half-grins formed on his lips, this time devoid of its early mockery and coolness. "Are you surprised I apologized?" And staring at him just as her heart started at the staggering truth—why, with his ruggedly cut features and too-long, chestnut locks, he really was quite—handsome. She forced her attention back to his words requiring a response.

"I am," she said stiffly. "Those I know do not apologize." Even as the words left her lips, she knew she'd just fueled his ill perception of her.

The man raised his glass to his lips. "That is unfortunate. An apology earned, is an apology deserved." He stared at her over the rim of his tankard. "Regardless of rank or status."

She would have to be as deaf as an adder to fail to hear the silent admonishment contained within those words. He was one of those who despised the lords and ladies for their birthright. In truth, belonging to that cruel, glittering world, she secretly concurred with his assessment of that Society to which she belonged. Cara returned her attention to her plate, effectively ending any further opinion from him on manners and kindness.

"Have you eaten a bite?" Humor laced those words.

"I have." She lied. The fork hadn't made it past her lips and she'd wager the heart contained within her trunks, left behind in the snow-covered countryside, that he knew as much, too.

He planted his elbows on the table and shrank the space between them. "Have you?" The man stretched out that last single syllable utterance.

Lifting her chin at a defiant angle, she took a bite. And promptly gagged.

"Then you are far braver than I, princess. I haven't touched a single serving of mine."

Cara choked on her swallow and grabbed her stained napkin. "You, sir, are no gentleman," she said around the fabric, glaring at him while he chuckled.

"I never presumed to be, pr—"

In a like manner, she dropped her elbows on the table and leaned forward. "Do. Not. Call. Me. Princess. One. More. Time." They locked gazes in a silent, unspoken battle, but she'd had so many years of staring down mean-spirited girls and whispering servants that she'd not be shaken by this bear of a man.

"Will."

She blinked in confusion. What was he on about?

There was a grudging respect in his eyes. "My name is Will."

She tested that name, running it through her mind. *William*—the name of kings and conquerors. It suited this man who issued orders and commandeered conversations between unfamiliar ladies and servants.

He continued to study her over his pewter tankard. "And does your station prevent you from sharing your name?"

She frowned. "Propriety keeps me from freely sharing my name." Except, as soon as the words left her lips, heat slapped her cheeks. Young ladies did not sit and converse with a stranger, in an empty taproom—and most especially without the benefit of a chaperone or escort. Speaking to this gruff man shattered the grounds of propriety in every way. His wry grin said he'd followed her thoughts, as well. "Cl—Cara," she quickly substituted.

Will winged an eyebrow upward. "And your title, princ—Cara?"

Triumph filled her at unnerving the bold man who'd chided her since she'd arrived. He'd expected her to supply her title and hold him to the bounds of propriety. A thrill ran through her at the audacity of this entire exchange; her being alone in the taproom of an inn with a man, challenging him and his expectations for her and of her. Since her mother's passing, she'd fit neatly into the mold designed by her father and Society. "What use would there be in turning the proper form of address over to a man who so disdains polite Society?"

He stilled and then tossed his head back. The tavern thundered with his laughter and she started, stealing a glance about at that shockingly bold sound of his mirth. Then, Will raised his tankard in salute. "Brava, madam."

Pleasure warmed her belly. He thought she was…amusing. No one thought she was anything beyond the…well, ice princess he'd taken her for.

His laughter died and his smile slipped. He worked his piercing gaze over her and lingered on her mouth.

Cara froze and touched her fingertips to her lips. "What is it?" Her question emerged with a hesitancy she did not recognize in herself. She picked up her napkin to brush it over her mouth once more. "Do I have something on—?"

He held up a powerful, olive-hued hand drawing her gaze to his long, naked fingers. "It was your smile."

She worried her lower lip. "My—?"

"It softened you," he spoke quietly, as though marveling to himself.

It softened you. Had those words been uttered by her father or the girls at Mrs. Belden's, they would have been tossed out as nasty jeers. Yet this man's low baritone wrapped that word in the gentlest caress, more beautiful than any effusive endearment. For with those three words, he'd plunged her into this unfamiliar universe where she craved a sliver more of the warmth his words had hinted at.

This weakening before him, a stranger who taunted her one minute and enticed her the next, roused fear at the power of her response to him. When most were content to avoid her, this man tempted and teased. Her chest tightened. People did not tease her. They did not compliment her. Not for any reasons that were kind, and only born of reasons that were cruel. Cara passed her searching gaze over his face. What game did he play? Annoyed at herself for believing for one moment that someone, somewhere might be so genuine as to like her for her, Cara set her lips and looked hard at him. "You seek to have fun at my expense, do you?" He opened his mouth. Not allowing him the opportunity to kill that joyful fluttering in her belly, she hopped to her feet and adopted the glare befitting the ice princess he'd declared her to be. "I do not know what business you have coming over here teasing me—"

Will came slowly to his feet. His tall frame dwarfed her smaller figure. "I am not teasing you." He spoke quietly, as though calming a fractious mare which only burned her ire all the greater.

Cara slashed a hand at the plate of untouched holiday fare. "Oh, and what was that earlier ploy to have me try the...the..." She wrinkled her nose. Whatever blasted food the innkeeper had plated her. "Food," she finished lamely.

He blinked slowly. "Well, that time I was teasing you."

Shooting a hand across the table, she waved a finger up toward his face the way he'd done upon their first meeting. "Perhaps you are bored or perhaps you are having fun at the expense of a lady of the peerage because you despise those of an elevated station." He snapped his eyebrows into a harsh, angry line. "But I neither want nor welcome being made light of." Then with years of regal pride drilled into her, she swept her borrowed skirts away, stepped around him, and marched from the cold, lonely taproom.

CHAPTER 5

Later that evening, Will lay abed. He shifted his frame upon the lumpy mattress and stared at the water-stained ceiling. With the hay-stuffed bed, he could certainly blame the miserable accommodation on his inability to sleep, and yet… He moved his gaze to the white, plaster wall. A faint sniffling came muffled through the wall and echoed off his hollow chambers. Yet, he'd be lying to himself. Since Cara, the lady without a surname, had stormed abovestairs with a grace befitting the ice princess, she'd held an unrelenting hold on his thoughts. A hold she'd easily maintained sharing the room beside him.

He should be grateful her stinging diatribe quashed his momentary captivation with that small, wistful smile on bow-shaped lips; lips he'd had a desire to crush under his. Which was madness. With the lady's icy cool and thoughts on station, she was everything he despised in women of her lofty status. Only the softness in her blue eyes and that tremulous smile on her full lips had transformed her into…a gentle, captivating beauty. There had been a hesitancy to her, an uncertainty that belied the unrepentant, chilled figure she presented to the world.

A faint noise met his ears. He strained to pull the noise in past the hum of nighttime silence. A sniffling. William stilled. Crying. There was a person crying. Nay—a young lady. The muscles of his stomach contracted. For his dislike of the rude woman, he'd sooner lob off his own arm than hurt one.

"B-bloody bastard."

Through the thin, plaster walls, her quiet weeping reached him. His gut clenched at the piteous sound of Cara's misery. *Christ*. He'd made her cry. Her earlier accusations against him came rushing back. The vise of guilt twisted all the harder. She'd taken him for a bully, and yet, with her weeping, this private window into her own hurt was more powerful than any words she might have hurled. He shoved himself to an upright position, swung his legs over the bed, and settled his bare feet upon the cold, wood floor.

"…I despise you…"

He winced. Just then he despised himself. Even if the lady had been ordering her servants about, he'd not see her hurt. Then, as though he'd merely conjured those tears of his own guilt, a black curse reached him.

"Bloody, codpiece-wearing, lice-infested dastard."

He froze. A grin pulled at his lips and some of the pressure in his chest eased. For his earlier annoyance with the pompous young lady, he far preferred this spitting and hissing, unrepentantly bold miss to the whipped and wounded woman she'd been a moment ago. "Whoreson of another whoreson dastard."

His smile widened. He knew the lady not even the course of an evening but he knew enough that if she'd found him listening in to her inventive curses that would have driven a king's soldier to blush, she'd take apart the wall and then promptly take apart him with her delicate fingers. His smile fell. He'd never known a lady to curse as this one did. That incongruity hardly fit with the flawless, rigid mold he'd placed Cara into earlier that afternoon. He furrowed his brow and stared contemplatively at the wall separating them. Perhaps there was more to the lady as the innkeeper had suggested. He caught his jaw between his thumb and forefinger and rubbed. Nor had he ever been one to form inflexible opinions of a person. He had, however, proven himself a rather good read on an individual. Such had proven a skill more than anything else in his traveling to distant countries and meeting people of foreign tongues.

His first read on Cara had been definitive—self-centered, self-important, emotionless lady.

And yet, seated across from him a short while ago, her eyes had sparked with an unguarded brightness that spoke of an altogether different woman…a woman who now wept in private.

"…miserable, rotted-eyed bastard…"

And who cursed like a sailor three sheets to the wind. Cara's words pulled a laugh from his chest. After endless minutes of having his ancestry and parentage called into verbal question by the cursing lady, silence descended. Then—

"Who is there?" The frantic, faintly panicked edge to that question carried into his room.

He remained frozen, staring at that thin plaster separating them. Following the lady's indignant march from the taproom, he'd sooner announce himself than he would march naked through the snow-covered hills outside.

The quick, soft tread of footsteps indicated the lady moved. Then a faint click sounded through the quiet inn like a shot in the midst of the blizzard. Bloody hell, the lady would wander alone, unchaperoned in the inn in the dead of night, no less? "Hullo?" she called, this time louder.

William bit back a curse and shoved himself to his feet. What if he were not the gentleman sharing her wall but some other bounder with dishonorable intentions, one who'd take advantage of her solitary presence and then claim the lush bounty that was her lips? Fury thrummed inside him while he closed the distance to the door in four long strides. A low growl rumbled up from his chest as he yanked it open.

Cara gasped and spun about.

"Are you—?" His words ended on a slow exhale and he froze in the doorway. He took in the lean, lithe creature clad in nothing more than a too-small nightshift that clung to her bountiful breasts. The garment climbed high above her ankles, exposing the delicate creamy white flesh. His gaze slid involuntarily closed. By God, she was the manner of beauty men waged wars over.

"Were you laughing at me—" The lady's indignant question brought his eyes open. "Again?" Cara stood, hands poised on her hips, with fire burning from her blue eyes and a wave of desire rolled through him as in her fiery stance, her shift pulled taut over her breasts.

"Laughing at you?" His words emerged hoarse. Had he? How could he ever laugh about one such as this tall, Spartan-warrior princess? And more, how could she have no idea he stood like a green boy before her, with lust raging through him?

She cast a glance up and down the halls and then returned her stare to his. Doubt filled her expressive eyes. "Someone was laughing at…m—" Cara pressed those bow-shaped lips into a flat line. *Me.*

Once again the lady fretted over the possibility of anyone smiling with her or about her. What did a lady who, by her birthright and beauty alone, likely commanded ballrooms, worry about people making light of her? That niggling question drove back the haze of desire that had cloaked his senses. To regain a footing in the world, where he was not this unnerved by a golden Athena who cursed like a thief from the Dials, he folded his arms and leaned against the doorjamb. Mindful of her maid sharing rooms on this very floor, he dipped his voice to a hushed whisper. "And do the opinions of others matter so very much that you'd leave your rooms in an inn with all manner of possible danger awaiting you?"

The first flash of unease lit her blue irises. Cara darted her tongue out and skittered her gaze about.

He narrowed his eyes. The lady believed him capable of harming her. Of course, she knew him not at all beyond their two previous meetings—both meetings which had been filled with plenty of jeering coolness on his part. He took in the faint tremble of her fingertips as she smoothed her palms over her nightshift and despised himself for giving her reason to be wary of him.

Cara followed his gaze downward and immediately ceased her distracted movements. All earlier indecision fled, replaced with the stoic calm befitting the lady who'd swept into the inn and made demands of her servants and the innkeeper. She gave a flounce of her hair. "Do not be ridiculous. I am not afraid," she raked her gaze over him, "of you." God, she was as bold and fearless as that Spartan princess he'd likened her to. "And," she edged her chin up a notch. "I hardly care what opinion people carry of m-me." There was a faint tremor to that last word.

William worked his gaze down the heart-shaped planes of her face, to the rapid rise and fall of her chest. Did the lady know she lied to the both of them with that hollow pronouncement? "Oh?" He gave her a pointed look.

Most every other lady would have looked away from the unspoken accusation he leveled. Cara tossed her head and glowered with an austere power that could be taught to future kings. Only, the icy look she adopted was effectively quashed when her untidy chignon tumbled free of the combs loosely wound in her hair. A golden waterfall cascaded about her shoulders, falling in rippling waves to her trim waist. Her eyes widened with the same manner of shock as if she'd just lost that ill-fitting nightshift. "Oh, blast." The lady quickly set to work gathering those silken tresses in her fingers.

He froze. His pulse thundered hard and fast, numbing his thoughts and blotting out sound as he stood, bewitched by this siren in white. In his travels, he'd earned the favors of some of the most skilled courtesans; wicked women in the finest satins, with experience in their eyes, and practiced fingers and movements. Not a single one of those creatures of falseness could hold a dimly lit candle to this lady's brightly burning, and more, guileless flame. Through her hopelessly futile efforts, he remained transfixed.

One of her hair combs slipped from her fingers and clattered to the floor, and startled him into movement. He gave his head a clearing shake and bent to retrieve the delicate, ruby piece, the same moment Cara bent forward. Their heads cracked together and the ruby heart fell from her hand once more.

"Bloody hell," she muttered and teetered sideways.

He quickly straightened and caught her against him, steadying her. They stood there still, their chests pressed against one another, moving in the same jerky rhythm. As a young boy, he'd been instructed early on of the perils of being alone with an unwed young woman; most of whom would have designs upon his title and, with those designs, could and would jeopardize the match his parents intended for him. In this moment, the lady could have had off with his future title and all the holdings that went with it, and he'd have handed them to her gladly for this moment. Will lowered his head and brushed his nose over the golden crown of her hair. The luxuriant tresses proved as satiny soft as he'd taken them for.

"Y-you sh-should n-not…" Her words, faintly breathless, came quickly as though she'd run a race.

The scent of her wafted over his senses—a heady, citrus fragrance that put him in mind of summer and purity. "I should not what?" he whispered against her ear.

"Touch you?"

The lady's audible swallow filled the quiet corridors.

William drew back and a small sound of protest caught in her throat.

DO NOT STOP. KISS ME.

Those shockingly improper, and all things sinful, words remained unfinished.

Never in the course of her entire life had she been this close to a man. Nay, *any* person. As the ice princess this man had called her not even six hours earlier, people did not speak to her, and they certainly did not touch her. When all the girls at Mrs. Belden's had whispered and chatted about those first forbidden kisses they'd received, a vicious envy had snaked through her—a desire to be that woman who drove gentlemen to dare conventions.

And now, standing in nothing more than her shift, in the powerful arms of this tall, virile stranger, eying her through his thick-hooded chestnut lashes, she felt—wanted. And there was something so very heady in *being* wanted.

William ran the pad of his thumb over her lower lip and her mouth parted slightly. "Cara mia," he whispered. His breath invaded her senses like a potent aphrodisiac made of ale and peppermint. "*Sei bellissima.*"

My Cara, you are beautiful. All those blasted Italian lessons she'd despised her father for insisting she take, worth every moment of suffering and tedium to have William wrap those words in his mellifluous whisper.

Oh, God. Her lashes fluttered wildly. No one had ever called her beautiful. Since she'd been scuttled off to finishing school, nothing but cruel words and mocking jeers had been leveled at her—words she'd been entirely deserving of. His husky baritone, wrapping about those Italian endearments, caused a warm fluttering in her belly that fanned out and raced through her.

He lowered his face so a mere hairsbreadth separated them and froze. For one agonizing, endless moment, fear spiraled through her that he'd draw back and she'd never, ever know the passionate kiss of a man who desired her for more than her wealth or status as a duke's daughter. Then she, who'd cloaked herself in a fictional strength and austerity, whispered, "Please."

As that entreaty slipped so easily from her lips, she stiffened. The reality of who she was and who he was, a mocking stranger who'd despised her for her birthright, intruded. He ran his inscrutable gaze over her face as the horrifying possibility that this was all some orchestrated game to bring her shame pebbled in her belly.

He palmed her cheek. "Please what?"

Her insides twisted. He'd have her beg? Her father would turn her out and disavow her birthright if he witnessed her pleading with a stranger for his kiss like some wanton harlot. She closed her eyes and leaned into William's hot caress. Her pulse raced wildly. Yet nothing mattered more in this moment, or any moment before this, than knowing his kiss. "Please, kiss me."

His body went taut against hers; the muscles of his chest tightened. Her nipples pebbled the front of her thin nightshift and the air filled with her quick, raspy breaths. For one agonizing moment built on this inextricable, all-consuming need, she feared he would deny her breathless request.

A groan escaped him as he crushed her mouth under his with the ferocity of a man who burned with the same hunger consuming her. She whimpered and, desperate to feel him against her, leaned up on tiptoe and twined her hands about his neck. With hard, determined lips, he tasted and explored the softer contours of hers. He slanted his mouth over hers again and again until a long, keening moan climbed her throat and spilled from her lips. William angled her closer and swallowed that sound by deepening the kiss.

A shock of charged power ran through her as he touched his tongue to hers in a first tender meeting and then an ever bolder, more demanding, caress. Her knees weakened and he easily caught her to him. He angled her so she was anchored between the thin, plaster wall and his tall, broad frame. Through his skilled movements, he never broke contact with her lips. William danced his tongue wildly in her mouth, as though he wished to learn the taste of her and burn it indelibly upon his memory, as she did him. Her heart hammered in her breast as she boldly met his thrust and parry.

As he drew back, a soft moan of protest stuck in her chest, but he only shifted his attention to the soft skin of her neck. "You worry I have been laughing at you, Cara *mia*. But the moment you smiled in the taproom, you captivated me."

His words ran over her like molten heat, this gruff stranger who murmured Italian endearments with the ease of a man from that country. "Will," she moaned. She dropped her head back presenting herself to his ministrations. He sucked at the sensitive skin of her neck and her breath caught in her throat. How could such a spot be so sensitive and elicit this wild thrill? The primitiveness of that masculine caress roused a pressure between her thighs. Heat pooled at her center.

A loud howling cut across their forbidden interlude.

He stepped away and quickly shot his gaze up and down the blessedly still-empty halls. The heightened storm outside matched the one raging between them even now. While he did a cursory search for interlopers, Cara pressed her hands to her chest in a bid to still her erratic heartbeat. Will returned his attention to her and the organ kicked up a frantic pounding, proving all her efforts futile.

If she were discovered in this *in flagrante delicato* manner with this man, not even of the same station, she'd be ruined. It would be the level of ruin no lady could ever recover from; the kind that would shame her family and leave her an outcast. And yet, she could no sooner step away from him than she could sever off her left littlest finger.

Powerful heat radiated from under his thick, hooded, chestnut lashes, momentarily stealing all logical thought. He broke the silence. "You should not be out here alone, Cara." Had his words been reproachful or mocking, she would have donned the cloak of rigidity she'd worn all these years. Instead, they were gruff, gravelly, and faintly pleading. Did she stir an inexplicable hunger in him, as well?

The possessive, and more…concerned glint in Will's blue eyes filled her with—a potent warmth—a desire to be closer to someone. Nay, not someone, him. To go through life with a person who cared for her and about her. A man who saw past her brittle smile and jeering comments to know that, inside, she was a woman who'd sell her soul to the Devil during Sunday sermons just to *be* cared for and loved. Then the reality of her existence intruded.

There would be no warmth and love. Not with the future someday awaiting her. The future being the eventual Duke of Billingsley her father would one day bind her to. That equally cold and indolent lord, who even now traipsed about the Continent, hadn't bothered with Cara since she'd been a girl of ten. Emotion lumped in her throat and a chill stole through her that had nothing to do with the ice-cold hallway and everything to do with the grim existence staring her down.

"Cara?" His gruff words rang with concern.

She drew in an unsteady breath. "You are correct. I will return to my rooms." Cara paused, lingering a moment. Her chest froze mid-movement with a hopeful anticipation he'd protest her leaving.

Instead, he remained stoic and all things coolly unaffected; a shadow of the man who'd taken her in his arms and given her, her first kiss. With head held high, she turned on her heel and marched the handful of steps back to her chambers, entered her cold, lonely rooms, and closed the door behind her. Cara turned the lock.

That thin, wood panel between them, she allowed her shoulders to sag and borrowed support against the door. She laid her head upon the aged, marred wood and silently shook her head back and forth. She'd always dreamed of that first kiss, but that explosive meeting had been the heady magic no wishing or fantasizing one could prepare for.

The soft click of Will's door closing filled her room and Cara caught her lower lip hard between her teeth. What she'd never anticipated was that one of Will's kisses would never be enough.

CHAPTER 6

FROM HER POSITION PERCHED AT the edge of her lumpy mattress, Cara sat with hands clasped upon her lap staring at the wood panel door—just as she'd been doing for most of the morning.

A gust of wind beat against her windowpane and she shivered as the breeze cut through the thin walls of the establishment. She cast a glance over to that frosted pane. The winter storm gave no sign of letting up and raged with the same kind of ferocity that had barred the earl's servant from recovering her belongings last evening. The precious pendant, that last link to her mother which mattered so very much, should occupy her thoughts and worries.

She'd never been without that piece once worn by her mother. So why was she thinking of something else? Nay, someone else. A very specific someone who, with his bear-like frame and long, strong hands, evinced the power of a man who worked with those hands. Will. The stranger who'd kissed her. She brushed her fingertips over her lips. A stranger who with his unerringly accurate words and charges had been more on the mark than any others in his assessment of her.

A knock sounded at the door. "My lady, can I assist you with anything?" The innkeeper's wife's concerned voice came muffled through the door and slashed through her troubled thoughts.

"I do not require any assistance," she called back, now for the fifth time since the woman had been arriving that morning. And still for the fifth time, a lie. She'd accepted new garments, also coarser, older, and smaller than a frame such as hers required. Beyond that, she wanted no one's company this day but her own. For with the solitariness of her thoughts, she could then put her world back to rights—a world where she was the frigid, proper daughter of a duke and everyone accepted that fact as truth.

Only she'd spent hours trying to reassemble herself and had—failed. For all the years of priding herself on her strength and unflinching aloofness, one forgotten carriage, and an evening at an inn had transformed her into this hesitant, uncertain figure she didn't recognize. And if she was at least being truthful with herself, she could readily admit she still preferred this pathetic creature to the reviled one all the girls at Mrs. Belden's gossiped about. And gossiped about with good reason.

Her half-sister, Mrs. Jane Munroe, slipped into her mind once more. Cara fisted the fabric of her borrowed blue skirts. She'd gotten the young woman sacked. She'd convinced herself that with the young woman, an instructor at her finishing school, gone then she could be free of the constant reminders of the manner of monster her father was. Instead, with those cruel, carefully delivered words to Mrs. Belden, she'd only proven that she herself was just as much a monster as the man who sired her.

Another knock sounded on her door and this time she was grateful for the intrusion into the guilt pressing on her chest. "Yes?" For the sliver of a moment, her breath caught in anticipation of Will on the other side.

"Would you care to come down for the afternoon meal, my lady? Or should I bring another tray?"

Of course it wouldn't be Will. What business had he at her door? Regret sank her breathless hope.

"My lady?" The innkeeper's wife prodded, insistence to her voice.

"Y-yes." At that tremulous quake to her words, she flinched. This is what she'd become. Cara lowered her hand back to her lap. "I'll take my meal in my room."

The faint shuffle of footsteps indicated the woman had moved. Except, with the snow pelting her small, lonely window, Cara furrowed her brow. Well, why in bloody blazes should she take her meal in her rooms? Again? Because some stranger she'd known just a day had cast this mad haze over her logical senses? She squared her shoulders. She'd not hide in her chambers. Not any longer. "Just a moment." With an alacrity that would have made Mrs. Belden glower, Cara came to her feet and all but sprinted across the room. She jerked the door open and rushed into the hall. "Wait!"

The old woman stopped and turned to face her with a kind smile on her lips. She started. People did not smile at her. Largely because she gave them little reason to. *Even though you've secretly hungered for even a scrap of kindness.* When she spoke, her voice faintly trembled. "I w-will take my meal below." Then striving for her smooth affectedness that protected her from the knowing in the old innkeeper's eyes, Cara tossed her head. "I've matters to attend belowstairs." Which wasn't altogether untrue. There was the matter of finding her borrowed driver and obtaining her trunks.

"Splendid!" The innkeeper's wife widened her smile and then without waiting for Cara to follow, made her way slowly down the remainder of the hall and to the stairs.

With the woman safely ahead of her, Cara paused and cast a furtive glance over her shoulder at the door next to hers. Was Will still in his chambers? She thrust away the thought as soon as it slipped in. Cara scoffed. A bold, commanding figure such as Will who'd quelled the words on her lips and ordered her servants about, was not one to hide in his chambers. Most especially from a lady such as herself. She wrinkled her nose and started after the innkeeper's wife. Nor for that matter was *he* the reason *she* was making her way downstairs. Only, she knew she lied. Even as that precious gift given her by her mother should be the focus of her thoughts, and not one of those pompous, powerful men who ruled the world, instead her mind and heart raced with an equally alarming speed with the memory of Will. And there it was again. That sentiment she'd been immune to all these years, visiting her not once, but now twice, since she'd arrived at this ramshackle inn—remorse.

As she descended the stairs and into the taproom, she resolved to be that woman she'd been all these years—one who didn't feel guilt or cry in her room or long for someone to care, if even in some small way. Cara knew how to be that woman; she'd been that empty soul since her mother died. She did not, however, know what to do with the maelstrom of emotions swirling in her breast since she'd left Mrs. Belden's. Her feet touched the hardwood floor and her gaze slid involuntarily about the darkened space. A fire raged in the hearth. Even for the earliness of the day, the storm battering the countryside cloaked the outside in thick, gray skies that barely penetrated the frosted panes.

She moved her gaze over the taproom. Her heart dipped. But for the earl's driver alone at a corner table, the room was empty. Will was gone. How else was there to account for his absence? *What reason had he to stay? Surely not for me.* Cara curled her toes into the soles of her boots and then looked about once more. He'd gone and would be nothing more than a memory…just like that last, tangible connection to her mother lying in the Godforsaken countryside collecting snow. Cara steeled her jaw. She thought not. Her gaze landed on the earl's driver.

The servant of middling years leapt to his feet. "My l—"

"Have you collected my belongings?" she cut in.

The man skittered his gaze about and then touched one hand to his chest.

Cara gave a brusque nod. Who did he think she spoke to? Or perhaps it was more he wished she spoke to someone other than him.

"Er…" He pointed a quaking finger at the front of the establishment. "It is still snowing, my lady."

Setting aside her earlier resolve to be the duke's cold daughter, Cara gave a wry grin. "Is it?" She infused a droll edge into her tone. Wind beat against the window. "Who knew it still stormed out?"

The driver blanched.

Alas, she'd never been lauded for her humor or her ability to elicit smiles.

A pang struck. Was that the effect she had on all people? Even those who'd known her but a handful of hours, and hardly at that if one considered their time together had been with him perched atop his box and her in the confines of the earl's carriage. Giving a snap of her skirts, she started for the groom, when Will's judgmental words pricked her conscience. "*You'd send a person out into this Godforsaken weather for your fripperies, brat…*"

Was it a wonder he'd have nothing more than a kiss and then be gone from her life as though she were…nothing?

She froze mid-step. The fire cracked and hissed noisily, punctuated by the ping of ice hitting the window. Cara squared her jaw. Will had taken her as one of those pompous, self-important ladies, but then isn't that how she'd gone through life these eleven years now? She remained unmoving, aware of the innkeeper and driver eying her with trepidation teeming from their gazes. Yet, she could no sooner speak or walk than she could displace her father from power and name herself duke. Since the loss of her mother, in a bid for her father's affection, she'd striven to be what he expected of her as a duke's daughter. She'd buried her spirit and all hint of emotion to become a perfectly flawless, rule-abiding lady. From the color and fabric of her gown, to the practiced smile on her lips, she'd given the world what they expected to see.

"My lady?" the innkeeper whispered, taking a cautious step forward.

Cara fairly twitched with the urge to break free of the *ton's* suddenly suffocating mold. Well, bloody hell, she'd not prove that kiss-stealing stranger correct. Not in this regard.

"I-I will see to your things, my lady." The servant grabbed the hat on the empty chair and stuffed it on his head. He started for the door.

She slowly straightened her shoulders. "No."

It took a moment for her words to register, but then the driver came to a slow halt. He stared perplexedly back at her. The driver tugged at his collar and shifted back and forth on his feet.

"That will not be necessary," she spoke in even, well-modulated tones.

A flash of surprise lit his eyes, followed quickly by relief. She peered at the window where the storm continued to rage outside. Cara scoffed. She'd not be daunted by a blasted snowstorm.

"You are c-certain, my lady?" he asked hesitantly, fiddling with the brim of his cap. The wary gleam in his eyes matched the look of one who feared he had his foot in a snare.

"I am certain," she said stiffly. She didn't require anyone's help to collect her belongings. Turning on her heel once more, she spun in a flutter of noisy taffeta and marched abovestairs to her rooms and over to the crude armoire. "Only think of myself," she muttered and jerked her wrinkled cloak free. She pulled the garment about her person and fastened the grommets.

With furious steps, she stomped out of the room, down the hall, and returned belowstairs, finding the driver gone. The man had likely taken his leave in fear that she'd return and put another request to him that would send him out into the storm. She did a cursory search for one particular man. Her heart dipped at finding him absent, still.

It matters not that I won't see him again. It matters not that he'll only live in my memory as my first kiss—and one man who'd not given a jot about my status as lady and challenged me in every way...

Ignoring the shocked stares of the old innkeepers, she made her way to the door and yanked it open. The sharp sting of cold sucked the breath from her lungs, momentarily stunning her. A howling gust of wind slapped her face with snow. Cara sputtered and dashed the flakes from her cheeks. Finding her breath, she stepped outside, and shoved the door closed hard behind her.

She burrowed in her cloak. "I found my blasted way here not a day ago, I c-can c-certainly find my way once m-more." Those whispered words echoed like thunder in the raging blizzard.

And then she started forward.

WILL STOOD AT THE WINDOW with his hands clasped behind his back. He stared out into the swirling storm, still raging. The violence of that powerful wind battering the leaden panes and the thick, gray-white, winter skies suited his mood. And where he'd previously mourned the warm kiss of the Caribbean sun on his skin, now he embraced the cold.

He was due home. It was, and always had been, an inevitability. He'd have to return to the world of sedentary lord who oversaw his future responsibilities as duke. And more...the time would come that he'd wed. Yet, the woman who occupied his thoughts was not the future bride his parents would bind him to, but rather, another—a lady who wept in private and cursed with an inventiveness that would have earned the praise of any wordsmith.

A woman he'd taken for an ice princess. *Cara.*

He let his arms fall to his sides and then scrubbed a hand over his face. That charge he'd leveled at the rigid lady one day earlier now mocked him. For in the quiet of the halls last night, while the world slumbered on, and the storm buffeted snow on the countryside, with her lips and whispered entreaties, Cara's molten heat could have eternally thawed the harshest winter.

He let fly a curse to match the ones the lady herself had uttered in the privacy of her chambers. In his years of traveling, and all the women he'd kissed, never before had one slipped into his thoughts and dug in with this tentacle-like grip. In large part due to the life he'd lived, traveling. There was no place for emotional entanglements. Even less place when there was a lady his parents would see him wed.

And after but a handful of meetings with the lady he'd first taken for the manner of cruel, unkind miss his future betrothed was purported to be, he'd been silenced by the very real truth—there was, just as the innkeeper had said, more to the lady than a mean-spirited mistress who ordered her servants about. *I have no right peeling back the layers to discover who the lady truly is…* For nothing could ever come of knowing anything more of Cara, the young lady who'd refused to give him so much as her surname. Another life awaited him. Just as another life awaited her.

Will curled his hands tightly at his back. His father had been far more lenient than any other duke ought with his son and heir gallivanting about the globe. How much of that leniency had been born of parental guilt at that unofficial, but not unspoken, contract they'd have him enter into with the Duke of Ravenscourt's daughter? He'd long resented the expectation for him to join himself with that woman. Though not one given to gossips, it would be hard to ignore the whisperings as they pertained to the woman his parents would see him wed. Words lent credence by his own father's confirmation about the lady's character. Still for that, his mother's bond to Lady Clarisse Falcot's late mother was such that she'd ask him to overlook a wife who was cold, cruel, and calculated because there was more there than any of Society saw of the lady.

He snorted. His mother had long been hopeful, seeing the best in all. He gave his head a shake. Those charges about a young woman, coming from her own godmother before she'd even made her Come Out were hardly endorsements where his future bride was concerned. And for two days he'd not given a thought to the grim future awaiting him, but rather the tart-mouthed lady who challenged him one moment, and the other moments eyed him with a soft, doe-eyed expression that could drive a man to madness.

For only madness could account for this hungering after Cara. From the windowpane, his packed saddlebags reflected mockingly back at him. That same insanity required he leave, winter storm and all. But twenty miles from his family's estate, the ride would be slow and arduous but hardly impossible. He sighed. A man who'd endured a trek in Nova Scotia during the heart of winter could certainly manage twenty miles or so by horseback. The longer he remained here with her, the more his world was thrown into question.

It was time to leave.

A sharp rapping at the door cut into his thoughts. With a frown, Will strode to the door and pulled it open. The innkeeper stood, worrying his hat between his hands. Concern glimmered in his rheumy eyes. A knot tightened in Will's stomach that came from years of intuitive preparedness of danger. "What is it?" he asked, when the man remained fixed in silence.

"It is the lady," the servant blurted. He continued on a rush, "She's gone out."

He cocked his head. By God, just twenty-six, there was no way his hearing was faulty and yet it had sounded as though the man had said—

"In the storm, my lord. She's gone out in the storm. And my wife urged me to go fetch you because the lady's driver is off hiding from the lady and I knew you could likely bring the lady back with a good deal more ease than myself—"

Another blast of winter wind shook the thin walls and William sprang into action. With the man still rambling on, he started around the wizened innkeeper and took off at a quick run. He clenched and unclenched his teeth as he surged through the narrow halls. The wooden floors groaned and creaked in protest as he bounded down the stairs and charged for the door. Will jerked it open with such force it shook the frame. Snow stung his eyes and momentarily blinded him. He slammed it shut behind him.

Fear warred with frustration in his chest and he fed all annoyance with the lady. For as he trudged through the snow, more than a foot deep, panic licked at him. He damned the high banks that slowed his pace. The bloody, foolish chit. What in bloody hell was she thinking? Did she not have the sense God gave an ant?

He squatted and the freezing snow penetrated his breeches, stinging his flesh with the wet cold. A pressure squeezed at his chest. What protection did the lady have? Her cloak and some too-thin gown she'd borrowed from the innkeeper? He ran his gloved palm over the small footstep left in the otherwise undisturbed snow. Will lifted his gaze and followed the steps as far as he could with his eyes, squinting into the thick swirl of snow. Coming to his feet, he then set out in pursuit of those smaller prints, footsteps belonging to a bloody, foolish chit.

What business did she have going out in—?

He came to a stop and narrowed his eyes. "Her belongings," he hissed. Will cursed again and then resumed his determined path for the lady. Fury ate away his earlier fear and he funneled it into that far safer sentiment. As he made his way to the road, he'd have wagered the joy he found in traveling these years, just where Cara had gone off to.

Sure enough, as he converged on a clearing a few moments later, the carriage pulled into focus. The doors hung open with the wind battering them. Cara stood perched precariously on the edge, with her gloved fingers straining for the black trunk atop. A thick haze of red clouded his vision. *This* is what the lady would risk life and limb for? "What in blazes are you doing?" he shouted into the wind.

Cara emitted a sharp shriek and flailed her arms. She crashed backward into a small drift and her bonnet flew from her head and sailed noiselessly into the snow.

"Cara!" Fear roughened his voice. Anger forgotten, he trudged the remainder of the way to the carriage, damning his strides slowed by the thick snow.

He reached her side. William braced for the vitriol in the young lady's eyes at finding herself indignantly sprawled in the freezing snow. Instead, a wide smile wreathed her face. That unfettered happiness sucked the thoughts from his head and he just gazed down transfixed. She lay upon the cold earth with her blonde curls blanketed about her and her sapphire blue skirts vibrant in an otherwise colorless landscape. Snow clung to her golden eyebrows and, but for the reddened tip of her nose, she may, in this instance, very well be the ice princess he'd professed her to be—magical and fey, she'd sucked the breath from his lungs.

Their gazes caught.

"Y-you s-startled me." All the lady's sure attempts at bravado were spoiled by the loud chatter of her even, pearl white teeth.

That snapped him to the moment. He cursed. "What in hell are you doing out here?"

She opened her mouth, but promptly closed it as he bent and picked her up. Through the dampened fabric of their garments, the crush of her breasts against his chest sent heat spiraling through him. Unnerved by this inexplicable pull, he cursed again. "You are so fixed on your blasted belongings that you'd risk your foolish life?" He set her down on her feet and she sank into the snow.

Cara nodded once. "Yes." She yanked the hem of her skirt up.

Ice slapped at their faces, leaving a painful sting to the flesh. Will ignored that slight discomfort. "Yes?" he seethed. Disappointment and anger filled him. For just then, he despised that she'd proven herself, once more, to be a woman to so value those useless items that sat atop her fine carriage. *So* cherish them that she'd place more value on them than her very life.

She nodded once more. "Y-yes." Had that tremble been attributed to unease with his sudden silence he'd be somewhat mollified. Except, she turned awkwardly in the snow and gestured to the top of the black lacquer carriage. "As you are h-here, would y-you be s-so good as to take down my trunk?"

Will narrowed his eyes. Why, she was out of her living mind.

CHAPTER 7

WILL WAS DISPLEASED. SHIVERING IN the snow with the wind buffeting her flimsy cloak, Cara took in the muscle ticking at the corner of his right eye. She fiddled with her skirts, burrowing into the largely useless fabric of her wet cloak. Nay, the man was a good deal more than that. She'd only once before bore witness to such disappointment and fury—the day she'd gotten her half-sister sacked from Mrs. Belden's, Mrs. Munroe had looked at her with a like expression.

She cocked her head. She'd been very clear as to what had earned the other woman's upset. Now, with Will, she could not account for the taut line of his mouth and his palpable fury. She widened her eyes. Of course. Given his lessons on proper treatment of servants, he'd expect some courtesy, on her part. "P-please," she blurted.

He puzzled his brow.

Humph. The lout expected more in terms of her gratitude. She inclined her head. "Will you *please* help collect my trunk?"

Will leaned down, shrinking the space between them. With a hairsbreadth of space between their mouths, her lips tingled with the fresh memory of his kiss. "Do. You. Think. I. Am. Angry. Over. Your. Lack. Of. Manners?"

By the manner in which he bit out those terse words, she'd wager not. Another gust of wind slammed into them and whipped the fabric of her cloak and gown against his leg. "You are d-displeased o-over something else?" She shivered, the winter chill seeping past the momentary warmth his nearness provided.

An ominous grumble climbed this fierce once-more-a-stranger's chest and stuck in his throat. Cara took several faltering steps back and stumbled over herself in her quest to get away from this glowering figure. She gasped and shot her arms out to steady herself. However, he only marched past. In one effortless move, he climbed onto the driver's perch and then hefted her trunk down.

It landed in the snow with a soft thump.

Emotion swelled in her breast. Ignoring the cold, she scrambled over and fell to her knees. Her fingers, numb from the cold, shook and she damned the uselessness of those chilled digits.

"Here," Will barked, pulling her attention up. He leaned down and, in one fluid movement, worked the latch open. "There," he spat. He slashed a hand furiously at her trunk. "Collect whatever it is that is so precious to you, princess."

She hesitated, as with that last, jeering endearment, he transformed her once more into that callous ice creature he'd taken her as…and with good reason. That unfeeling lady she'd been groomed into after her mother's passing was, in fact, the person she truly was. With that angry truth, she fished around the neatly folded gowns of white satin. Where in blazes was it? Her heart thundered in a panicky rhythm as she sought that hidden pendant. Then her fingers collided with the hard metal and she sent a prayer skyward. With tremulous fingers, she withdrew the necklace. The ruby, a crimson mark of vivid sadness upon the stark, white winterscape, tugged at her.

"Ah, so *that* is why you'd risk your life." William's regret-tinged words brought her neck back with such alacrity she wrenched the muscles.

She winced. And where he'd judged her before and been correct in his harsh suppositions, in this he was wrong. He saw her as nothing more than a lady, enamored of her precious stones and gems. William held an arm out and effectively quashed the defensive rebuttal on her lips.

"Come," he said gruffly.

Silently, she wrapped one hand about his arm and curled her other around the last gift she'd ever been given. They moved slowly.

Cara's breath came fast, stirring the winter air as she labored to lift her foot from the wet snow and take another step. She'd no doubt Will could run the distance to the inn without so much as an extra breath taken, and yet, he remained at her side—a woman, who by the sneer on his lips and glint in his eye, he clearly despised.

They broke through the copse of juniper trees and the inn pulled into focus. "Why?"

Cara didn't pretend to misunderstand. "I'm greedy, Will," she said, giving him the truths he expected. She leaned against him in a futile bid to steal his body's heat. "I- I could not sleep all night in fear of my cherished diamonds." Pain stabbed at her heart. That was how little he thought of her. And why shouldn't he? What manner of avaricious creature had she proven herself with her orders to the earl's driver a day earlier? The world saw a person the way one might through a frosted pane; hazy and blurred, distorted.

He brought them to a stop. "It was a ruby."

He'd noted that small detail. She fisted the heart pendant in her hand. The edges of that stone bit painfully through the fabric of her glove. "And there were other jewels and a trunk of satins and silks."

Those miserable pieces paid for by her father. She hated everything and anything connected to the vile reprobate—including herself who by the very nature of blood made her an extension of that foul figure.

She looked at Will squarely. His face may as well have been a mask he'd donned, so little she could tell from his expression. "It was," she said tightly. Or rather… "It is a ruby." He pierced her with his gaze and with the intensity of his stare, he may as well have looked inside and plucked all those sorry pieces of her existence and made them his. No one had ever looked at her so closely. No one. It left her open and vulnerable, filled with a tumult of emotions she didn't know what to do with. Her feet twitched with the urge to flee. Cara made a hasty move to step around him.

Will placed himself between her and escape, effectively blocking her forward stride. For one of his impressive size, he moved with a surprising agility. Cara folded her arms close to her chest and hugged herself tightly, praying he attributed that small protective gesture as a bid to find warmth.

"Why?" he asked quietly.

Why should he ask? Did he see a glimmer of the person she'd once been and secretly, with the tiniest sliver of her soul, wished to again be? One who felt and loved and longed to be loved in return? She bit the inside of her cheek hard. "Why does it matter?" That raspy question tore from her throat.

He palmed her cheek. Cara longed to jerk her chin away and shake free of his intimate caress. With his tender touch, he threatened to shatter the carefully constructed defenses she'd built about her heart.

"It matters." That low pledge rumbled up from his chest.

Oh, God.

Perhaps the sliver of her soul that craved warmth was far stronger than the rest of her cold, miserable self, for she ached for him to keep touching her in this soft, searching way.

After her mother's death, Cara had retreated into herself. The perils in sharing anything personal had been made clear when, as a girl, her own father had rejected that offering. "Why?" She turned a question on him. Her mind warred with the need to give Will details about her past and those intimate parts of her pathetic life story.

For a long moment, she expected he'd ignore the query she put to him in return.

But then, he passed that penetrating gaze over her face and lingered on her eyes. "I took you to be a self-centered lady."

Bitterness surged in her breast. "I *am*." Those were the truest words she'd ever spoken to another person since her mother's passing.

Will dipped his head and layered his brow to hers. Their breaths mingled and the puffs of white escaping each of their mouths melded as one. "Do you know what I believe, Cara mia?"

Cara stood immobile, as frozen as the sharp icicles hanging from the sign outside the inn. She could not so much as muster nod. "What?" Her breath emerged as a breathless whisper.

"I believe there is more to you than you'd have people know."

How could this man see so much of her when the world saw nothing more than the icy façade she presented? The part of herself that had spent years keeping people out wanted to lash out at him for his knowing. Yet, for the first time in more years than she could remember, no stinging diatribe sprung from her lips.

"What do you see?" she whispered, aching to know, and more, be that person he took her as.

"I see a woman who loves to smile but who fears doing so." With his words, he reached inside her heart and fanned that long-cold organ with a contagious warmth that spread its beautiful heat to other parts of her too-long chilly being. "I see a woman who is so very afraid of being whispered about and talked of that she presents an empty, unlikeable façade to the world."

The unerringly accurate words speared her. She parted her lips in silent shock.

He brushed his thumb over her lower lip. Of their own volition, her lashes fluttered and then drawing in a deep breath, she let him in. "It was my mother's."

WILLIAM STILLED, HIS THUMB PRESSED to Cara's full, lower lip.

It was my mother's.

Not is. *Was.* Pain dug at his belly, as with the glimmer of sadness in her expressive eyes, Cara's dogged tenacity in collecting her belongings now made sense. As though unnerved by the thick silence between them, she stepped away.

She unfurled her small hand. The crimson ruby stood vivid on her kidskin gloves. "The clasp is broken." To demonstrate as much, Cara fingered the intricate and clearly damaged clasp. He studied her head bent over the piece. "It was my mother's," she repeated, the murmur so very soft, the winter wind carried with it nearly all sound. "She died when I was seven."

At the faint tremble of her fingers, the evidence of her stoic grief, pressure weighted his chest, making it difficult to draw breath. How could this woman, a mere stranger two days ago, and one he'd not much liked upon first meeting, have caused this dull ache, as though her pain was his?

Her eyes grew distant and by the sad, little smile on Cara's lips, her mind danced back to those times when she'd been happy. "My father insisted I don only diamonds." She gave her head a wry shake. "I despise them. I could not understand why anyone would wish to wear those clear, colorless stones. Not when there are far more vibrant and interesting gems."

The wind tugged at her bonnet strings and knocked it backwards on her head. With the burden of her necklace in her hands, she attempted to right it. William reached for it.

Cara recoiled. "What are you doing?" She eyed him warily.

Ignoring her, he unfurled the long, red ribbons and carefully lifted the velvet bonnet. He set it atop her riot of golden curls. His movements slowed by the chill in his fingers, William retied the strands underneath her chin.

"Th-thank you." Was the tremble to Cara's words a product of his touch or the winter cold?

The rules of propriety rang in his ears, urging him for the first time since he'd entered this inn to turn on his heel, escort Cara safely back, and then leave as fast as his mount could possibly carry him. "Then how did your mother come by the ruby?" he asked, instead, his tone gruff. How much easier it had been when she'd been nothing more than the materialistic, grasping lady who valued her personal belongings before the lives of her servants.

"Oh, it was her mother's," she said with a matter-of-factness that raised a smile. "My mother said I should wear it and always remember there is far more beauty in being colorful than in…" She let her words trail off and looked past him.

William captured her hand in his and raised it. "Than in what, Cara?"

She unfurled her palm, displaying that cherished piece. He stared at the crimson heart. "Than in being a colorless piece that inspires no emotion in anyone." She spoke of herself. Is that truly how the lady saw herself? How could a woman who'd charge into a dark hall to challenge a person she'd believed laughed at her, or stalked off in the midst of a storm to rescue her own possessions, not see the strength of her own spirit?

"Forgive me," he said quietly.

She opened and closed her mouth several times like a fish floundering on shore.

"Again, Cara, are you surprised I am capable of an apology?"

Cara shivered and then hugged her arms to her once again. "I am surprised *any* man would be capable of such."

He frowned. As with that admission, and the story of her heart pendant, she let him inside a world she'd lived. A world where her father had sought to quash her spirit and churn her into a cold, vapid lady whose sole purpose was the match he'd no doubt make from her. By her bold actions at the inn these two days, the man had tried and failed. And with that revealing piece, she once again threw into question everything he'd believed about her.

I am an unmitigated ass.

He steeled his jaw. "Never bind yourself to any such man who'd try and kill that colorful part of who you are." His words came out gruffer than he intended. For as soon as the words left his lips, an image slithered in of some faceless, nameless bastard who'd lay claim to her body and attempt to purge the happiness from her soul to be nothing more than a polished hostess. A lethal desire to end that imagined man for daring to possess any part of her burned through him. He staggered back and the cold momentarily sucked the breath from his lungs. For how else was there to account for this inability to draw air?

Cara studied him in that silent, assessing manner of hers. Something sparked in her eyes—regret, sorrow, resignation, and then her expression grew shuttered.

And he *knew*.

Knew before she so much as uttered them, what the words poised on her lips would be.

"My future has already been set for me."

His stomach muscles clenched. He couldn't, not for eight more years of freedom granted by his father to travel and avoid that shrewish lady waiting for him, force out the question.

She studied her palms. "My father has selected the perfect," her lips twisted in a macabre rendition of a smile, "nobleman for my husband."

He had no place caring. Though no formal contract yet existed, another lady waited for him and Cara would exist as nothing more than the tart-mouthed beauty who'd ensnared his attention. Even knowing that as he did, he wanted to kill both her father and that lord who'd received her cold sire's approval. A shudder wracked her lean frame and snapped him from the red haze of fury blinding his vision. "Come," he said gruffly and held out his hand.

Cara eyed his fingers a moment and then slid her palm into his. He folded his hand over hers and even through their wet gloves, a charge of heat penetrated through and shot pinpricks of desire running through him.

Wordlessly, they walked the remaining way to the inn in silence.

And before, he'd not wanted to leave this ramshackle inn for the future awaiting him. Now, as he opened the door and Cara slipped inside breaking that contact, he found himself not wanting to leave for the past that would remain behind here.

CHAPTER 8

FROM WHERE HE STOOD AT the hearth, William cast another glance at the stairs. The faint, aged contralto of the old innkeeper's wife sounded behind him and he glanced back. A collection of greenery littered one of the inn's tables and she quietly sang as she worked.

Oh! how soft my fair one's bosom,
Fa la la la la la la la la
Oh! how sweet the grove in blossom,
Fa la la la la la la la la
Oh! how blessed are the blisses

He joined his baritone to her ancient voice.

"Words of love and mutual kisses,
Fa la la la la la la la la."

Martha widened her eyes and stopped mid-song. Surprise sparkled in her eyes. "You know the Welsh song then, my—" She stopped just shy of that proper address.

William winked. "I spent one Christmastide season in Wales and learned the lyrics to *Nos Galan.*"

She nodded slowly, approval in that subtle movement. With a jaunty hum of the same tune, Martha returned her attention to her bough.

He pulled out his watch fob and consulted the timepiece. Did the lady plan to sup in her rooms? Of course, that was the proper thing for a lady to do without the benefit of a brother or chaperone's protection and he didn't doubt Cara had lived the better part of her life conforming to be that proper English miss. Still, disappointment filled him at the prospect of not again seeing her.

"I expect she will be down soon."

William spun about. "Hmm?"

Martha sat with her head bent over the wreath while working the threading of her sewing needle with gnarled fingers. "I expect your lady," she said not picking up her gaze from her efforts, "should be down shortly." She tied a wrinkled, red satin bow about two branches, connecting the evergreen. A smile played on the woman's lips. "And her coming will have nothing to do with the lady's leaking ceiling." She picked up her head and spoke on a conspiratorial whisper. "Even if she tells herself it is."

A dull heat climbed up his neck and he resisted the urge to yank at his collar. He, who'd never struggled with words, came up empty when presented with the older woman's knowing look. Had he been so very transparent in how each moment spent with Cara had drawn him more and more under her spell?

Since early that morning, when they'd parted, he'd not been able to rid his thoughts of the golden-haired beauty. Of what she'd shared. Of her past. Where most young women of eighteen were filled with a carefree innocence and hope, her light had been dimmed by the darkness she'd known at her father's hands. Through all their exchanges, however, there had been the flicker of light and spirit, and it would kill him the day their paths would eventually intersect once more at a *ton* event when he was the proper duke's heir and she was the frigid, unapproachable lady he'd first met in this inn.

The fire snapped and hissed noisily. William balled his fists. He'd not think of a world where that was again the woman she became. He'd remember her as she'd been, lying on her back in the snow, joy dancing in her eyes and etched on the delicate, angled planes of her face as she stared up at him. From where she sat working on her Christmas bough, Martha cursed drawing him to the moment. A small smile pulled one corner of his lips. And he'd forever recall Cara as the lady who cursed with an inventiveness possessed only by a poet's turn of phrase. He made his way over to the table. "Did I mention I had a good share of experience making Christmas boughs?"

She looked up with a glimmer of surprise and, in an assessing manner, took him in. A twinkle lit her rheumy eyes. "I would wager a charmer such as yourself has a good deal of experience with the kissing boughs, hmm?" She waggled her stark white eyebrows.

He winked, eliciting a laugh from the old woman. She motioned to the colorful bows and fabrics scattered about her table. "I've but the three branches for the boughs." He followed her sad gaze over to where her husband shuffled with pained movements about the taproom. He pushed the broom over the dusty floor. "Every year we would go out and collect the green together." Her eyes lit with a blend of happiness and sadness converging as one with that old memory. "How very fast time goes. You are making those boughs one Christmas to kiss your love and the next," she held up her gnarled hands, "and the next you cannot even make your fingers move."

The passage of these eight years was testament to the rapidity of time. What would he have become thirty-eight years from now like this aged couple? Where they knew love and joy in their marriage, his would be a cold, calculated affair that, if he was fortunate, would bring him children and very little misery. "Here," he said quietly.

LATER THAT EVENING, HER WET garments cast aside for another borrowed dress from the innkeeper's wife, and the chill gone from her jaunt into the storm, Cara hovered at the base of the stairs outside the taproom.

Since her return, every last thought had belonged not to the misery of being the unwanted, unloved, and often forgotten daughter of the Duke of Ravenscourt, or the misery staring down at her if... She gave her head a shake, *when* she wed that pompous, also unfeeling, future duke. Instead, Will had laid claim to her every thought, so that her skin still tingled with remembrance of his touch, and her heart yearned to speak with him once more.

Heart racing, Cara peeked around the wall with the same surreptitiousness she'd shown as a girl listening on silently while her mother wept in the privacy of her rooms. She took in Will's exchange with the old innkeeper's wife. What manner of man was he? One who spoke Italian with the ease of one who'd lived there for the whole of his life and also sang Welsh carols with an equal fluency alongside the old servant. She fought to swallow past the emotion in her throat as she continued to observe him speaking to Martha. *Martha.* Not the innkeeper's wife. Not a servant. But a woman whose name he knew and whom he spoke to with such kindness and gentleness that went against the cruelty and pomp- ousness evinced by her father.

Fear stuck in her breast. With trembling fingers, she grabbed the bannister and pressed her back against the wood. She'd prided herself on needing no one. She'd convinced herself that she nei- ther wanted nor cared about the opinions, thoughts, or feelings of another person. Cara slid her eyes closed. The world shifted under her feet with the staggering truth—she craved that connection with Will. She wanted a man such as him in her life; a man who saw past the surface to the woman she was, a man who wanted her to be *real*, and not flawless and fake.

Cara drew back and dropped her desolate gaze to the shadows that danced upon the floor, cast by the taproom hearth. This fledg- ling bond to another soul was a potent aphrodisiac, shown her by a stranger, no less. She touched her lips and heat burned through her. Though, was Will truly a stranger? How could he be when he'd been the first man to challenge her, and kiss her, and whom she'd shared those most pained, intimate memories of her mother with?

She forced her hand back to her side as regret turned inside her. Ultimately, however, that is what Will was. He was a stranger who would ride out on his horse to… She swallowed hard. To where she knew not because she knew nothing of him. Nothing beyond how he made her feel and what he made her wish for. And she could not, nay, would not, go through the rest of her life without knowing more of him than those insufficient pieces.

That forced her into movement. With resolute steps, Cara stepped into the taproom. From where he sat working alongside Martha, he stilled. His broad shoulders tightened the fabric of his black jacket. With the smooth elegance carried by kings, he shoved to his feet and turned.

His powerful frame filled the suddenly small taproom. Cara dimly registered the old woman rising and then dropping a curtsy. The glow cast by the hearth illuminated the knowing glimmer in the woman's eyes as she slipped away. Heat warming her cheeks, Cara slid her gaze over to Will. Her attention slipped to the bulge of William's triceps straining his coat sleeves—the cut and color best suited to a gentleman of polite Society than a man whose callused hands and tanned visage bespoke a life different than the foppish dandies about town. Oh, goodness. She fanned herself and then followed his gaze to that telling gesture.

Cara swiftly dropped her hand to her side. From under his thick, dark lashes, Will stared across the length of the small space, singeing her inside and out with the heated desire to taste more from his lips.

You are not to speak to anyone who is inferior to you, gel…is that clear?

But who is inferior, Your Grace…?

Everyone who is not kin to a duke, prince, or king… Now get from my sight. I've matters to attend…

A log shifted in the hearth and exploded in a spray of orange and crimson sparks. Years of the stiff, regal reserve drilled into her at the hands of those nurses and instructors hired by her father echoed around her mind. Cara smoothed her palms down the front of her skirts. Abandoning every last ostentatious thought she'd ever carried, she walked forward. With each step, the chains of propriety slipped loose until she came to a stop several steps away from him, free in ways she'd never been before—until him.

She tipped her head back to look at him. He studied her in that inscrutable manner. Cara curled her hands into fists as a sea of indecision lapped at her. Yes, he'd kissed her until their breaths had melded in the same, desperate rhythm but beyond that had any of their exchanges meant anything to him? Doubt needled her mind. She took several faltering steps away.

"Don't," he spoke quietly, bringing her hurried retreat to an immediate stop. Passion burned from the depths of his fathomless eyes. "I want you—"

And God help her, she wanted to know that burn. Her heart caught in a splendid way. "What do you want?"

"Ah, my lady, you've come to take the evening meal!"

No! Cara spun about and swallowed back the swell of disappointment over the innkeeper's untimely interruption. *What?* She silently pleaded with Will. He wanted her to join him for supper? He wanted to discover more of who she was inside? What did he want? *Mayhap he wants me to go....* After all, but for her mother, who'd really ever wanted her around?

Her skin pricked from the curious attention trained on her by Martha's husband. Cara forced her lips to move. "I have," she said stiffly. She shifted her gaze from Will and looked to the older man. "That is, I would very much enjoy taking my meal belowstairs."

"Splendid," he said with a burgeoning smile.

She took several steps, following the innkeeper, and then stopped. Her heart thumped loudly at the shocking proposition rushing through her head. Ladies did not humble themselves before men. Daughters of dukes humbled themselves before no one. "Will you join me?" she blurted. Heat scorched her cheeks. Never in the course of her life had she so humbled herself before another human being. She felt exposed and bare and wanted to throw her head back with exhilaration and flee all at the same time.

Silence met her inquiry. That painful moment may have been a minute or a year for as long as it was. Only, as he studied her in his assessing way, she ached to call back those revealing four words. The sting of his rejection would wound her in ways her father's antipathy never had or would. For her father had seen her more as an inanimate extension of himself, that could be used to advance his wealth and prestige. William had seen the cold exterior and challenged her at every turn, defying her to be something other than that ice princess, daring her to be more.

Cara bit the inside of her cheek hard and hurried after the innkeeper when Will placed himself in her path. Her breath caught painfully at the raw strength of him. This was no satin knee-breech-wearing dandy. Will was the manner of man who would put warriors of old to shame. He lowered his head and, when he spoke, his words came out as a low, gravelly whisper, so faint she wondered if she dreamed his response.

"I want to join you, Cara."

The innkeeper hurried over to pull out a chair for her and she claimed her seat.

The whisper of reason cut across her private yearnings. "I should not be here," she said faintly, as the innkeeper rushed off. Will froze with his hand on the back of his seat. "We should not be here," she corrected. For with each meeting in this taproom, and each stolen exchange in the halls and countryside, she risked ruin.

He hesitated and, for an agonizing moment, she thought he'd leave; knew when no one had ever been there, largely because they'd not wanted to be with her. "Do you want me to leave?" he asked instead.

Cara tipped her head and blinked slowly. Decisions had been made for her through the years. Expectations thrust upon her. Now, this man would give her the freedom of her own decision and it was heady stuff, indeed. Her reservations melted away. Her father and his plans for her could go hang. She smiled hesitantly up at him. "I do not." She drew in a breath and, just as she'd begged for his kiss last evening, now she'd be willing to cast out the remainder of her pride, just to be near him. "I want you to stay."

In one fluid motion, he pulled out the chair and claimed the spot across from her. He motioned the old innkeeper over and held up two fingers. "Two tankards of mulled cider." As the older man rushed off to collect the requested drinks, Will folded his arms at his chest and looked back at her. Never taking his gaze from hers, he looped his ankle over his opposite knee.

Cara studied the broad expanse of his muscled chest; the way his muscles strained the fabric of his jacket. She gulped. No lord she'd ever met possessed this man's masculine, powerful rawness. With a silent curse she jerked her attention up, praying he'd not observed her scandalous appreciation of his form.

The ghost of a smile played about Will's lips, proving the Lord was otherwise busy this evening. "You wished for my company, Cara. Now, what would you care to discuss." He rolled his shoulders and his muscles once more strained the fabric of his expertly cut jacket.

A slight frown pulled at her lips as she examined that jacket for an altogether different reason—that evidence of his wealth. What was *his* story? "Who are you?" she asked, the words spilling from her lips.

He cocked his head. Then, his expression grew guarded and he eyed her with the wariness of a pickpocket who'd brushed his side. "You already know who I am. My name is Will—"

She slashed a hand through the air. "I know your name, but not even the full of your name." And if he left now, how would she ever again find him?

I won't, you blasted ninny. We belong to very different worlds. And in the world already shaped and crafted for me, my father would have me belong to another. And panic added an extra rhythm to her heart. These two days were not enough. They could never be enough. And yet, they had to be.

He took a slow, infuriatingly casual sip from his tankard. "So, you intend to divulge your identity this night, as well, *my lady?*"

But why? Why did it have to be enough? Why could she not steal more for herself, for the first time, ever?

Will quirked an eyebrow.

Her cheeks warmed. How was he so unaffected when her world teetered back and forth in this confounding way?

Another splash of heat burned her neck and climbed up her cheeks. "That is different," she muttered.

"Perhaps," he said, noncommittally.

She steeled her jaw. Regardless, the information she sought of Will moved beyond a mere name. She wanted to know who he was under this sometimes darkly dangerous, sometimes gentle, stranger. The innkeeper's wife rushed over, interrupting their exchange. She set down two plates of…? Cara wrinkled her nose. Something. There was definitely some kind of food heaped upon the plate.

Dismissing the woman with a look, she propped her elbows on the wooden table and leaned forward. For the first time in the course of her adult life, she asked something she never had before. "I want to know about *you.*" She gestured to the table of evergreen branches and satin ribbons. "You speak Italian and know songs in Welsh. You will sit down and help a woman with inane decorations for the holiday season. How do you know all those things?" How, when she knew so very little about the world beyond the tedious, proper lessons ingrained into her? Envy sliced through her; a desire to have lived a life of more—and more terrifying, a desire to live that life with him.

WILLIAM STUDIED CARA FROM OVER the rim of his glass. She asked who he was. What would the lady say if he were to tell her he was, in fact, heir to a dukedom? That title, nothing more than a chance twist of fate, had defined his future. It mattered to all women who saw nothing more than the title. What would she see? "I have spent the past eight years traveling," he said at last.

Cara scrambled forward in her seat. "Traveling?" she whispered with the awe of a woman who'd discovered herself in possession of the queen's diamonds. Then her eyes formed round moons. "With the hue of your skin, you've the look of a man who travels distant, warmer seas." She paused and flared her eyes. "Are you a pirate?"

He chuckled. "I am not a pirate." How could he have imagined the pinch-mouthed miss who'd coldly ordered her servant about would now boldly speak of his skin and dream of pirates?

Her eyes hinted at her slight disappointment. The lady longed for excitement and hungered for more in her constraining world. How very much alike they were in that regard. Something pulled at him under the weight of that realization. Cara prodded him with her gaze. "Where have you been, Will?"

He rolled his shoulders. "Ireland, America, Canada. France, Italy."

In an endearing little move, she rested her elbows atop the table and dropped her chin on her hand. "I've been nowhere outside of Mrs. Belden's and my father's dratted estates."

William quirked an eyebrow. "Mrs. Belden?"

She wrinkled her nose like she'd had a sniff of Martha's latest fare. "A finishing school," she mumbled. "This is my last year." By her earlier telling reaction about that finishing school he'd expect more than the forlorn sag of her shoulders.

She was to be married to a man chosen for her by her unfeeling father. Was it any wonder she should wear her sadness like a cloak upon her person? He raged at the mercenary world they belonged to.

Cara picked her fork up and stabbed at the piece of flank. She continued to wear that resigned look in her eyes. Desperate to restore her to the exuberant young lady she'd been prior to the mention of Mrs. Belden, he nodded to her dish.

"Is it dead?"

Cara blinked several times and then looked to the questionable contents upon her dish. She snorted. "I daresay it is too soon to tell." They shared a smile and then she inched closer to the edge of her seat. "If you are not a pirate…" She gave him a hopeful look.

"Which I am not," he repeated, grinning.

"Then what is it that has you traveling so much?" She'd clung to her questioning which was only heightened by the excited light in her eyes.

It was not what he'd been in search of, but what he had been fleeing from, that accounted for his travels—a woman. An arrangement awaiting him. Darkness settled on his thoughts, but he promptly shoved it back. He'd not let thoughts of Clarisse sully this moment.

Martin came over and William gave thanks for the timely interruption that saved him from formulating a response. "Here you are, my lady." He set down one tankard of cider before Cara and then another for William. "My…" The old man cleared his throat and then turned with a surprising agility and left.

With Martin gone yet again, Cara this time remained stoically silent. Had she correctly interpreted his absolute lack of desire to talk about his circumstances? How wholly selfish of him, when he wished to know everything about the paradox that was Lady Cara. She fiddled with her tankard, looking anywhere and everywhere. This uncertain side of her, so at odds with that coldly aloof stranger who'd marched through the doors and put demands to the servants and servers here. Then she stopped suddenly and looked at him squarely. "I want to know more about you." All the audacious boldness in that admission was ruined by the becoming blush that stained her cheeks.

William leaned back in his seat and the wooden chair groaned under his shifting weight. Drink in hand, he continued to assess her. "You want to know about me?" he asked, cautiously. For the span of a heartbeat, he believed she'd discovered the truth. That somehow she'd deduced that he, William Hargrove, was, in fact, a marquess and future duke. But then she gave a hesitant nod, hinting at her reluctance in such daring questioning. "What would you know?" he asked slowly. More…why did the lady care? Why, unless this mystifying pull that had sucked at his thoughts and self-control gripped her as well. And what madness was it that he wanted her to feel this off-kilter captivation from his presence, too?

She wetted her lips. "I paint." Cara whispered it the way a young woman speaking of a tryst with a lover might. Her admission brought him up short. Then, wasn't the lady always doing that to him? "Or I used to." The lady prattled when she was nervous. Tenderness filled his heart over that intimate discovery. Then a serious glimmer darkened her eyes. He ached to lean across the table and take her in his arms, shoving back that solemnity she'd demonstrated at their first meeting, two days ago. "My father let my governess go for daring to encourage such unladylike pursuits," she spoke softly, her tone befitting one who'd only just remembered that dark, sad memory.

Once again, the urge filled him to hunt down her blasted tyrant of a father and knock him on his noble arse. He gripped his tankard hard.

Then she started and gave her head a sharp shake. "Do you paint?"

He shook his head. "I do not." William grinned and gave her a wink. "Not well."

A sharp, startled laugh burst from her lips and once again the air froze in his chest. When she laughed, small silver flecks danced in her eyes and an aura of unjaded innocence etched in the planes of her cheeks in the form of a faint dimple. And he wanted her always to be this way. For this was Cara; not the brittle, angry lady who'd stomped into the inn yesterday.

"I have three siblings. Two brothers and a sister," he said gruffly.

"Do you?" Surprise lit her eyes.

William nodded. Siblings he'd seen but only a handful of times in the past eight years. How much of their lives had he missed in his thirst for adventure? Regret rolled through him. He took another drink, grimacing at the bitterness of the mulled cider.

"Are you the eldest?"

He nodded. "I am." The ducal heir. Oh, he wished Oliver or David had been granted that right. For then, in this moment, he'd be unattached to the woman his parents would bind him to and free to find that elusive sentiment of love.

"I have an older *brother*." That slight mocking emphasis she placed on that last word, said more than any charges she might level about the man.

He'd wager all his happiness that her childhood had been a lonely one, with a disapproving father and detached brother. But still he clung to the hope that her upset stemmed from an overprotective, needling sibling. "Are you close with your brother?"

She eyed him as though he'd gone mad. "There is no warmth in noble families, Will." Regret contorted her features. "Every aspect of a lord and lady's life is devoted to rank and status with little regard for one another's hopes or dreams." The woman spoke with the sage tone of an ancient master instructing a young student.

Words stuck in his throat. What would the lady say if she knew he not only belonged to the cold, merciless world she spoke of, but that he'd also been the recipient of love and affection in a household filled with exuberant laughter? "I cannot believe all families are as you describe. Surely there is, at the very least, some happiness to be found?" For the alternative was a dark, cold, lonely world for her in a way that twisted at his heart.

Cara shook her head. She picked her fork up and shoved it about her plate of beef and potatoes. "You would be wrong," she said with a matter-of-factness that again wrenched his heart. She motioned to herself. "The only purpose served by children is to advance one's rank and status and so those emotionless entangle-ments are formed."

With her one-sided cynical views of all noble families, in this her words proved accurate. He stared blankly at her golden curls arranged in a loose chignon on the nape of her slender neck. His parents, even as they knew a grand love, had been bound by an arranged marriage, with love only coming later. As such, they would bind him to Lady Clarisse with some misbegotten expecta-tion on his mother's part that he would also find love in a like way.

His dark fate looming before him, he could not ride away from this inn and have Cara accept that cold, empty fate for herself. He needed her to know there could be happiness and warmth and laughter. William leaned forward and covered Cara's fingers with his. The satiny softness of her skin burned his larger, callused palm with a sharp heat.

She stilled and, for a long moment, examined their joined hands. Did she wish to commit this moment to her forever memory, as he did? Then she met his eyes. The muscles of her throat moved.

"You deserve far more in a future than the world you speak of. Not all families are like yours, Cara." He infused earnestness into his tone. "There is laughter and teasing and happiness."

A sad smile formed on her lips, with evidence of her earlier iciness, and he braced for the hint of that aloof lady from yesterday. But then she looked to the frosted window. Her eyes grew stricken. "The storm has ended."

The absolute quiet for the first time in two days filtered through this stolen interlude. He followed her stare. Indeed, it had. And with the cessation of that thick snow, he could soon be on his way. The moment he rode out, they two would each live their lives and their time here would exist as nothing more than a too-brief moment in time. Regret and panic merged as one, clawing at him.

"I…" She shoved back her chair and hopped to her feet with such alacrity, her seat nearly tipped precariously and then righted. Did she see that their time had come to an end and she would be off with her maid and driver to the pompous betrothed who'd, no doubt, shape her into the lady Society expected her to be…crushing the fledging spirit that had stirred these past days. Ah, God, that inevitability gutted him until he wanted to snarl and howl. Cara's hands fluttered about her chest. "Of all the places you've been, if you could go anywhere, in this moment, where would it be?"

He stood. The irony not lost on him. Since his return to England, he'd dreamed of being anywhere but here. And now… He couldn't drum up a single place he'd traveled or longed to visit that he'd rather be just then. Cara probed him with a look, her eyes begging him for an answer he didn't have. He searched his mind and gave her the place he'd show her, if the circumstances of life and fate had been altogether different. "The isle of Capri," he said quietly. "It has water a shade of blue you did not know existed and skies to match. The sun possesses warmth that cleanses a person's soul."

The muscles of her throat worked. "I would very much like to see that place," she said hoarsely.

Do not go. Dishonorable words he had no right thinking with the pledge he'd made his father eight years ago. "Cara," he said quietly. She bowed her head and then silently fled. He stared after her, hungry with the need to call her back. William looked to the frosted panes. Yes, the winter storm had ended. And yet, an altogether different tempest raged inside.

CHAPTER 9

CARA DESPISED MORNINGS. PARTICULARLY THE cold of winter mornings. She preferred to burrow deep into the feather down of her bed and snuggle under her coverlets, absorbing the warmth and dream. Dream of painting and dream of being far away from Mrs. Belden's cheerless rooms, and even farther away from her father's lonely halls. In the brief moments before she arose and greeted the truth of her existence, those fantasies belonged to her.

This morning, she despised above all others. But she despised it for altogether different reasons. Cara stood at the widow and stared at the smooth surface of the untouched white snow that gleamed from the sun's bright rays reflecting upon it. A pressure weighted her chest and threatened to cut off her airflow. She leaned her forehead against the cool pane; the sun's warmth penetrated the glass at odds with the cold. Those once jagged, fierce icicles dripped a steady stream into the ground below.

And this stolen interlude, this momentary reprieve from the cold world in which she lived, and peoples' disdain of her, and her disdain for herself, was at an end. She was once more the Duke of Ravenscourt's daughter; hated by all, reentering the hallowed halls of that loathsome man who'd sired her. A sheen of tears flooded her eyes, and whereupon her arrival at this place days earlier, they'd been a token of weakness that she'd despised herself for showing, now she embraced those drops which blurred her vision. Her shoulders shook with the force of her sobs. Her forehead knocked noisily against the window.

This was what came of forgetting her station and flinging propriety into the wind for the company of a man. Nay, not just any man—Will. Only, he'd penetrated that carefully crafted veneer; a façade so convincing, she'd come to believe it herself. And now that he'd shaken the foundation of her artificial world, she could not reconstruct the wall and put the pieces of her former self back together. Cara cried all the harder.

How naïve he'd been with his talk last evening of a loving family who cared. That was not her world. That was his. And she hated him for making her hunger with this desperate ferocity for a sliver of it—but not just with any gentleman. With him. A man whose last name she did not even know. A man who'd forced her to look inside herself and confront that she'd become a person she detested, and wished to be…someone different.

Cara allowed the tears to freely fall and then drew in a shuddery sigh. "Enough," she whispered. She dashed her hands across her cheeks. Will would leave. Today, no doubt. And she would board the earl's carriage and be off to the father who'd forgotten her and the brother who may as well be a stranger for how well she knew him. Another sob burst from her lips and she stifled it with a hand. "I-I cannot." To return to her father and Mrs. Belden would mean her eventual descent into marriage with that someday duke—just another man like her father. One who'd crush what little remained of her spirit and force her into the Societal mold expected of a lady. She stared blankly at the earl's driver in the distance as he made his way from the stable yards to the inn. "I-I cannot," she whispered to herself, fisting her hands at her side. She needed more time. And with jerky movements, spun on her heel, quietly pulled the door open, and collided with Alison.

Despite her wan complexion, Alison wore her perpetual smile. "My lady." She dipped a curtsy, but then her cheer dipped as her eyes went to Cara's cheeks. "My lady?"

Cara averted her face from the girl's concerned stare. "Alison, you should be abed." And once more she was the selfish Lady Clarisse, for she wished Alison to the rooms so that she might have another taste of that beautiful freedom she'd known these days. That precious gift withheld from women.

"I am fine, my lady." She eyed Cara's rumpled gown with a frown. She made a tsking noise. "Come, my lady." With her usual boldness, she stepped past Cara. "The earl's man has fetched your trunks. Allow me to help you into another gown."

Of its own volition, her hungry gaze moved beyond Alison and into that hall. Then some of the fight slipped from her being and seeped out her feet. She gave a curt nod and moved with wooden steps back into the room. Her maid entered and closed the door behind them, closing off that path to freedom.

The young woman cleared her throat. "I-I..." She shifted on her feet, looking anywhere and everywhere except at Cara. "I am so sorry," Alison murmured. "I sh-should have been seeing t-to you and I understand you must speak to His Grace about my failing to see to my responsibilities." She gulped loudly.

What would the young woman say if she discovered Cara had not been hidden away in her miserable, private rooms as the other girl supposed, but rather taking her meals in a public place, without the benefit of a husband or chaperone or father? It was the level of impropriety that would ruin her for anyone...

"It is fine," she said at last. The look Alison gave Cara proved that she knew her failing to attend her responsibilities was not fine. Or to the duke it would not be. "We will not speak of it again." *Someone will inevitably find out.* There were the innkeepers. Though they did not know the truth of her identity, the earl's driver, in fact, did. He'd seen her in the tavern. Alone. Speaking to Will.

While Alison rushed about the room, tidying the space and collecting a change of garments for her mistress, a defiant smile pulled at Cara's lips. Would it truly be such a very bad thing if the pompous nobleman her father would see her wed discovered that the proper, propriety-driven daughter of a duke had been alone at an inn, with a man? Her lips burned. A man whose kiss she'd begged for and still craved. A kiss she would continue to crave until she was an old woman, alone, with nothing more than the sweet memories of these few days.

In an uncharacteristic silence, Alison helped Cara from one gown and into another. Then with skillful fingers, she set to work pulling at and arranging her curls into some semblance of a proper chignon. As she tugged at the strands, tucking them into the butterfly hair combs, questions spun through Cara's mind.

How could her maid not know while she'd been healing in her rooms, Cara's entire world was flipped on its ear by a stranger who'd challenged her at every turn?

"There you are, my lady."

The girl's wan pallor indicated how much energy her efforts had cost her. Guilt pulled at her. "You need to rest," Cara said softly, leading her back to her rooms.

The loyal maid widened her eyes.

"What is it, Alison?" Cara asked.

"You are… you are…"

She gave her head a shake, urging a suddenly taciturn Alison to finish those words.

"…being kind."

You do not apologize. You do not speak to servants. You are not kind to them. They are your inferior in every way. Is that clear, Clarisse…?

Her father's even, disdainful tone echoed around the chambers of her mind.

Shame filled her at the shocked confusion in her maid's tone. Cara managed a wry smile. "Well, it is never too late for a person to learn something new." She followed her words with a wink that elicited another weak smile from the girl.

Will had wrought havoc upon her ordered world. Only this disorder, which had set her adrift at sea, was the exhilarating type that made her want to toss free the shackles that had bound her all these years. They'd reached Alison's rooms and Cara helped her inside. Cara paused in the doorway. An apology earned, is an apology deserved… "I am sorry," she said softly.

Alison furrowed her brow. "My lady?"

"I have not been kind to you through the years and…" She caught the inside of her lower lip between her teeth. "…and for that I am sorry." Her toes curled reflexively into the soles of her boots at those humbling, unfamiliar words on her lips and before the young woman could respond, Cara hurried from the small rooms and closed the door behind her.

Inside the hall, she eyed the steps and then looked at the stairwell at the opposite end of the floor, just past Will's rooms.

Will.

Her throat spasmed and with desperation driving her movements, she made her way silently down the hall, hesitating a moment outside his rooms. Cara pressed a kiss to her fingertips and then brushed them over his scarred door. And then she continued on to the stables.

WILLIAM STOOD AT THE WINDOW. With the frost now thawed from the glass, it left a watery trail, sad and sloppy in its wake. He brushed his hand over the pane, clearing the moisture, and leaving the mark of his blurry palm print.

His packed saddlebags reflected in the crystal while the fierce sun beat down on the snow covered ground and roads. It was time to go. He closed his eyes a moment. Just days ago it had been the lady facing him at the end of that proverbial road who'd made it impossible to finish the journey home. Now, he could not force his legs into movement to finish this journey for reasons that had nothing to do with his future betrothed and everything to do with Cara. Only, this make believe world they'd allowed themselves to believe was real would ultimately end this day.

The time would come, by the very nature of his station and hers, that their paths would again cross. A future duke and a lady betrothed to some priggish, English peer would one day again meet. The air left his lungs on a swift, broken exhale. For the moment that would be—they would each be wed to their respective matches with the intimacy of these past couple of days a secret memory they would share, breathed aloud by neither, existing only in their minds.

I can offer for her...

The tantalizing thought slid in and, for a moment in time, he grasped on to that scandalous and yet enticing possibility. He cursed and as soon as the words left his mouth, a broken laugh escaped him with the remembrance of Cara's secretly scandalous tongue. Which only roused tantalizing memories of the contours of her lips.

William swiped a hand across his eyes. What hold did she have over him? Upon their first meeting, he'd not even liked the lady. But then, he'd looked closer, under the practiced façade. Truly looked. And what he'd seen underneath was a woman who'd known loss in her mother and battled years of coldness at a remote father's hands. A woman who'd been instructed to be that which Society expected of a proper English lady, who'd adopted that icy exterior to prevent herself from pain. The hurt flashing in her blue eyes, however, was the powerful emotion belonging to a young lady who felt a good deal—and who fought hard to suppress any and all emotion. No doubt in a bid to make herself immune to further hurts. Deep inside, however, dwelled a woman who longed for more.

And God help him, he wanted to forsake the pledge he'd made his father about the duke's daughter and be the man to give Cara more.

He pulled at his lapels. But it could not be. If he did not leave now, he'd be only further drawn into the seductive spell she'd cast upon him. He turned, just as a flash of green caught his eye. With a frown, William looked on as Cara took wide, lurching steps forward into the still-deep snow. He skimmed his gaze about for sign of her servant or driver, for anyone…but found the grounds empty. Periodically, she would steal a glance around and then with a final furtive look about, she disappeared inside the stables.

He scrubbed his hands over his face. *She is not my business. Soon I will be off and she will remain behind, and carry on with her life, and I will carry on with mine and…* "Bloody hell." William spun on his heel and strode across the room.

The chit didn't have a blasted brain in her head. He jerked the door open so hard it shook on its hinges. Fury thrumming through him, William marched from his small, rented chambers and walked purposefully through the short hall. He took the stairs quickly and then, ignoring the lady's driver who sat taking the morning meal, exited the tavern.

As he stomped a path to the stables, the birds sang a maddeningly cheerful tune. His boot steps churned up the icy snow as he followed the trail of Cara's smaller footprints. With each step closer, fury built in his chest. What in blazes was the lady thinking? Did she not have the sense to realize what peril awaited her? Then, as a sheltered, protected lady, she didn't know the dangers that existed—unscrupulous men who'd not hesitate to steal her innocence. A growl climbed up his throat and he continued on to the stables.

"Bloody hell."

Her whispered curse cut through the doors and brought him to a stop. Despite his annoyance, a grin split his lips. William quietly shoved the door open. The rusted hinge screeched in protest. It took a moment for his eyes to adjust to the dimly lit quarters. He scanned the area and frowned. Why, it was as though she'd simply vanished. He whipped his head about, searching for that golden-haired temptress who'd laid claim to his thoughts. Where in blazes had she—?

"Goddamn you."

That caustic loathing in Cara's words froze him. He shot his gaze to the floor where she lay with the upper portion of her chest tucked under the carriage. With violent, angry movements, she shook the axle to the black lacquer conveyance.

He creased his brow as another stream of mumbled ramblings flooded the stables. All the angry fury that had sent him marching to the stables drained from his tautly held frame. He scratched at his head. "Are you trying to break your axle?"

His words brought Cara up quickly and she cracked her head under the base of the carriage. Scooting out from under the frame, she sat up. Her hair tumbled down about her, falling free of her loose chignon, and he went still. His breath stuck a moment at the erotic sight of her and that curtain of blonde hair draped about her, as it drew forth tantalizing images of her, naked upon his bed, with those tresses wrapped as a silken curtain about their entwined bodies.

Christ. Disgusted with himself, William forced himself into movement. He flew across the stable and fell to a knee beside her. His chest tightened at the evidence of her physical pain. "Are you hurt?" he demanded.

Cara rubbed at her head and winced. "I am fine," she said and then ruined the matter-of fact tone by cringing.

William dragged forth the panicked concern that had sent him running after her. "What are you doing?" he asked again, and then lowering her arms to her side, set to work inspecting the bump at the top of her head.

She winced as he touched the red flesh. "Ouch." Cara favored him with a frown. "I was…" She flinched again as he continued his search. "Must you do that?"

"Yes," he said without hesitation. William probed the flesh, already darkening to a purplish-black. "You've bruised your head."

"And my pride," she muttered.

Ah, Cara. How carefully she guarded her dignity and emotions. "Why were you attempting to break your carriage?" A feat she, no doubt, knew impossible and yet attempted anyway. His gut clenched. What desperation drove those actions?

She shrugged off his touch and came quickly to her feet so that for a brief moment, with him kneeling at her feet, she had the advantage over his tall frame. "What would you have me say to you?" she demanded, her tone sharp. "That I tried to break the bloody carriage? That I would rather return to miserable Mrs. Belden's than my own home because there is nothing for me there?"

Oh, God. Her words ran ragged through him, twisting the knife of pain at the sight of her suffering. A muscle jumped at the corner of his eye and he stretched a hand out. "Oh, *Cara mia*."

She ignored that offering and he let his arm fall to his side. "I do not want your pity," she spat. "I neither want it n–nor need it." Her attempt at aloof disdain was ruined by that faint tremor. And with her revelation, the mask she'd donned at last made sense. Cara sought to protect herself. She'd been so hurt and broken by those who should have loved and cared for her that she'd transformed herself into a person who sought to bury all emotion. That realization only gutted him all the more.

"I do not pity you," he said quietly. He ached for her hurt and would make it his own if he could, but never pity.

With angry eyes she searched his face. Then wordlessly, she presented him her back. She wandered over to the carriage. Her shoulders shook in a silent expression of grief and he'd rather be run through than witness the sight of her suffering.

William strode over and settled his hands on her shoulders. She stiffened. If he gave her softly whispered platitudes, she'd reject them. "If I could take your pain and make it my own, I would own all this hurt and every other you've known leading up to it," he whispered against her ear. Cara's shoulders quaked all the more. He placed his lips against her temple and allowed her the freedom of her tears. They remained there, with their presence taunting the fates into an eventual discovery. William wrapped his arms about her and drew her back against his chest. He braced for her rejection, but then she folded her arms over his and leaned into him.

"My father forgot me."

For a moment, William's ears tricked him. "My father forgot me," she repeated and those words were spoken more to herself.

"He forgot you?" he managed to squeeze out past tight lips.

At her brusque nod, he swallowed down a black curse. What father forgot his child? Even in his years of traveling the Continent and the Americas, his father and mother's missives had invariably found him. Letters with words of love and pride and questions of his travels. The manner of family Cara spoke of was a foreign one to him. Knowing Cara's own life had been devoid of such familial love caused a dull, throbbing ache in his heart. William curled his hands tightly and she winced. He forced himself to relax his grip. "When?" Emotion gave the query a gruff undertone.

She shot a look over her shoulder at him. "N-now." Cara wrinkled her nose, and he'd wager his future title of duke that her tremulous reply was not a product of the cold. "Well, n-not now." With quaking fingers, she ran them over the gold crest emblazoned on the carriage. He took in the snarling lion. "This is not his seal. This is not his carriage."

Confusion rang in his ears. *Not his seal?* "I do not understand," he said slowly, attempting to follow her disjointed explanation. He opened his mouth to ask the identity of the bastard who'd so callously forgotten her; *needing* to know the name of that miserable sire. But the stark pain in her eyes quelled all words and the moment passed. For in this moment, knowing that man's identity would not erase the pain Cara now knew; the pain she'd always known.

"This is a carriage loaned by another young lady's father after *my* father forgot to send his 'round to Mrs. Belden's." A mirthless laugh spilled from her lips. "He, no doubt, wished me to spend my holiday at the empty school, where even the head dragon despises me."

Vitriolic hatred spiraled through him for the man who'd sired her and then subsequently forgotten her. An unholy, powerful urge to find the man and take him apart with his hands momentarily blinded William. While he'd spent the past eight years of his life resenting his father for expecting him to wed the Duke of Ravenscourt's daughter, he'd still been permitted freedoms and assured of his father's love. Where had Cara's happiness in life been? Where had been the person to love her and care for her? He ceased rubbing her shoulders and gently turned her around. Bold and unabashed as she was in every way, she squarely met his gaze. "You deserve more," he said quietly. "You deserve to love and be loved. You deserve to laugh and know there is no shame in feeling."

Her lower lip quivered and she lifted up her palms. "What does it say of me that my own father cannot love me?"

Had she taken a sword and splayed his heart open, it could not have hurt more than this piercing agony ripping through him. Emotion graveled his voice. "It says nothing of you and everything about him." A man he'd gladly throttle if he ever had the misfortune of meeting him. *But I won't. My words will never again collide with hers after this Christmastide interlude.* Pain stuck in his stomach, dragging the air from his lungs.

"Perhaps," she said noncommittally giving him a sad smile. "But perhaps not." She gave a toss of her curls. "Not that it matters. Christmas is really just any other day of the year. There is nothing so very special in it."

Memories flitted through his mind. What the holiday season had been like for him as the Duke of Billingsley's son—the laughter, the celebration, his one-time child's excitement for Cook's Shrewsbury cakes. He'd sell his soul on Sunday for the right to show Cara that it didn't have to be the cold, lonely time of year.

As a taut silence fell between them, William accepted he could not ride out this day as planned. Not with all she'd revealed and not with the truths she'd shared. More than ever, he wished to spend the remainder of his days showing her that every day was one to be celebrated. He leaned close and touched his lips to the lobe of her ear. She tipped her head and opened herself to that subtle caress. He took her by the hand. "Come with me."

"I thought you were leaving," she said but allowed him to pull her from the stables and outside into the snow. Her teeth clattered noisily. A light gust of wind whipped the fabric of their cloaks together. Her words pealed with hope and relief and a joy ran through him that shouldn't even matter.

"Not yet," he said helping her through the drifts, ignoring the painful bite of the winter's chill. William guided them away from the stables and off to the juniper trees in the distance. They stepped into the copse, where the snow-covered trees enveloped them in privacy. He released her hand and crouched.

Cara folded her arms and rubbed them, as though trying to bring warmth to her chilled limbs. "Wh-what are you doing?" Cara asked as he gathered snow into a ball.

He glanced up and his chest tightened at the tracks left by her tears. William managed a half-grin. "Don't tell me you've never made a snowball."

She eyed it and then looked questioningly to him. "Never."

He made to rise, but her words brought him up short. "Never?"

Cara shook her head and dislodged several golden curls. She stopped rubbing her arms and gave her gloves a tug. "My father wouldn't dare permit such inanity." Her mouth tightened.

He gave thanks for the restoration of her spirit that blotted out her earlier misery. Oh, he'd no doubt her pain went far beyond those handful of tears she'd silently cried, but she deserved to turn herself over to all those emotions—the anger, the hurt, the resentment, the pain. "When I was a boy, I'd throw rocks in the summer and balls of snow in the winter when I was upset."

A sound of annoyance escaped her. "I am not upset. I am m-merely c-cold."

His lips twitched at her indignant response. "Of course," he replied solemnly. "Regardless…" He held out the rounded missile.

Cara wrinkled her nose, reddened from the cold. "I am not throwing a snowball, Will."

He quirked an eyebrow. "Because ladies do not hurl snowballs?"

"Prec—oomph," She widened her eyes as though she'd received a pistol ball to the chest and glanced at the smattering of snow left on her cloak. "Why…why…you *hit* me."

"With a snowball," he amended. "You need to release the tight reins you have on your control." From where he squatted, he hastily assembled another and hurled it at her skirts.

Cara stepped out of the way, but the snow slowed her movements and his missile found its mark. If looks could burn, she'd have melted the snow with the outrage in her eyes. "S-stop. Hitting. Me. With—" He tossed another and it connected with her abdomen. "That is quite enough," she muttered and stooped. With quick, angry movements she made a—

A laugh burst from him. "What in blazes is that?" He jabbed his finger in her direction.

She pursed her lips and stole a glance about. "What is what?" Then she followed his gaze to her misshapen snowball. "Th-this is a snowball," she said with the same indignation she might if he'd questioned her parentage.

William snorted. "That is most assuredly *not*—" Cara drew her hand back and hurled her poorly constructed missile. He easily leaned out of the way and it sailed past. "A snowball," he finished.

A flurry of inventive curses split the quiet as she set to work building another snowball. She wet her lips and then eyed the object in her hand. With a beleaguered sigh, she held the snowball up for his inspection. Pride warred with uncertainty in her eyes.

He eyed the rounded ball and gave a slight nod of approval. "That is much imp—" She tossed her weapon made of snow, but it sailed into a sad, quiet heap several feet in front of him. William waggled his eyebrows. "Tsk, tsk, you are not very good at this, my lady."

Her teeth chattered. "I-it is b-because this is silly. It is f-freezing and wet out."

"And those are excuses." he said folding his arms at his chest.

"Th-they are not excuses." She stomped her foot and then cursed, shooting her arms out to keep from tipping over. "F-furthermore, throwing a rock or a snowball will *n-not* make me feel better."

William strode over to her, taking in the flecks of silver hurt dancing in her eyes. He stopped just a handbreadth a way. "It is not about making you feel better, Cara." The wind whistled and a loose golden curl danced over her eyes. He brushed it behind her ear.

"Th-then what is it a-about?" she gritted out between her clattering teeth.

Leaning close, he whispered against her lips. "It is about feeling something and feeding that emotion. You are angry." She opened her mouth as though to protest and he gave her a look, which silenced her. "And you should be. No father should forget his daughter." Rage slithered around inside him so that he wanted to hunt her father down and bloody the man senseless for having hurt her; with his abandonment and in his unfeeling treatment of her through the years. "There is no shame in feeling." He bent once more and made another snowball. Standing slowly, William held it out for her.

They stood locked in a silent battle of wills and then tipping her chin up, she took it from his hand. He positioned himself at her back. "You require a target." He looked about and then gestured to the trunk of a wide juniper. "Draw your arm back. Further," he urged when she hesitated. "Do not break the movement as you follow through with your throw and then with all the anger you have for your father—"

"I am not angry," she bit out, letting her arm fall. "I do not care that he forgot me." Her earlier unspoken grief stood testament to that lie. He'd not, however, strip her of that dignity.

"Hurl it at the tree," he continued as though she'd not spoken.

Her long, beleaguered sigh stirred the cold air. "Oh, very well." Following his instructions, she tossed the snowball. It sailed to the left of the tree trunk. "There, are you happy?" she snapped. "Now are we d—"

William gently wrapped his hand about her forearm, halting her retreat. How many years had she spent retreating from the emotions roiling through her? "I am not happy. That was a pathetic attempt." She pursed her lips. How hard to go through life concealing who you are and what you felt—even from yourself. He held her gaze. "You need to turn yourself over to feeling, Cara."

HIS WORDS WRAPPED ABOUT HER like a lover's seductive kiss. He waved that tantalizing glimmer of...*feeling* and challenged her to embrace that part of her, inside, that was very much alive. Emotion filled her breast. How long had she feared being mocked or judged? In her life, the girls she'd had the displeasure of knowing and even her father's servants had delighted in her flaws. So much so that she'd sought to be the perfect ice princess William had taken her as.

The old anger and hurt of her father's disdain rushed to the surface and, with it, the years of solitude and silence she'd endured in a household where she may as well have been invisible to her brother. *It is unbecoming for a lady to cry even after her mother's death...*

With a raspy growl climbing up her throat, she bent and made a flawless, rounded snowball then sent it sailing into the tree trunk. It collided with a loud, invigorating *splat*. Taken aback, Cara's mouth fell open and she looked from the powdered residue left as proof of her victory and then to Will. He stood at her side, a gentle, encouraging smile on his lips. "I-I did it."

"Of course you did," he said and stooped forward. He constructed another missile and held it out.

She claimed it without hesitation. "This is for forgetting me," she called at her inanimate object. She tossed another ball and it found its mark.

William proffered another ball.

"This is for not allowing me to paint." She tossed another. Her chest heaved with the force of her exertion, but the winter air purified her lungs, spreading its cleansing, healing power through her once-cold being. He continued to supply perfectly molded snowballs.

"And for binding me to a man just like you." This time, Cara bent and assembled her own. "And I am *nothing* like you," she shouted into the quiet. Only, as she threw, she no longer knew if the furious energy lending her strength came from the sad, sorry little girl she'd been, alone in a loveless world, or the bitter, angry, friendless woman she'd become.

She threw until her arm ached from her efforts and her breath came fast and hard. And then she stared at the juniper with its branches drooping under the weight of its melting burden. With the tension drained from her, the humiliation of letting Will into her world burned her with the heat of shame. Never had she allowed anyone entry in this way and suddenly she hated him for exposing her. And more, she wanted to be so exposed with another person.

She ground her teeth. "I am not taking part in this any longer. This is silly," she complained and snapped her skirts. Only, as she spun on her heel, she propelled with such force in the uneven snow that she flopped backward.

A startled shriek escaped her and she flung her arms out to prevent a fall. Her efforts futile, Cara landed in an ignoble heap on her back. She closed her eyes and braced for Will's laughter and when he did, she would never forgive him for forcing her into opening herself and then finding mirth in her retreat. His boots ground the snow in a noisy manner as he strode over. He lay down alongside her, their shoulders pressed together. She opened her eyes and turned her head slightly to look at him.

He remained with his gaze fixed at the shelter of trees above. "It is beautiful, isn't it?" he whispered. The blue of the morning sky filtered through the branches.

Cara managed a nod, but then recalled he could not see her with his stare trained as it was. "I-it is." Coldness ran through her. It left her hollow and desolate and had nothing to do with the icy snow penetrating the fabric of her lined cloak and everything to do with the truth that she'd never again see him.

Wordlessly, he came to his feet, and then held a hand out.

Cara wanted to snap and hiss at that offering, and a couple of days ago she would have sneered words of disdain for that gesture. Now, she placed her fingertips in his gloved palm and allowed him to help her stand. "You will leave today?" She prayed he accounted that faint tremble to the cold of the day.

Will lowered his mouth to hers and brushed his lips over hers once. "I must."

Of course he must. She nodded jerkily, but the swell of tears in her throat made words impossible. It was he who ended this last stolen moment of bliss she'd ever know.

Another lingering wind rustled the trees overhead and sent snow falling to the earth.

Their chests moved in like movements; swift and hard. "We need to return." Reluctance underscored Will's low baritone.

"Yes." They should have never stolen off into this hidden place and yet she'd gladly trade her respectability and good name to be here with him now.

He dipped his head and brushed his chin atop her hair. "If we are discovered, you will be ruined," he whispered into the tangled mass.

Yes, that was true and, at one time, such a thought mattered. No longer. Cara leaned up and pressed her lips to his. He went immobile as she kissed him and with a groan, he wrapped his arms about her, pulling her close to his chest. He made love to her mouth with his, as she'd longed for since that silent night in the empty hall of the Fox and Hare Inn. She angled her head, learning the taste of him—mint and mulled cider—committing all of him indelibly upon her memory so she might carry it with her always, into the long, cold, lonely future awaiting her.

Their embrace was one of panicked desperation. Her breath rasped wildly and she twined her hands about his neck. Will opened his mouth and swallowed those shamefully hungry sounds. This was not enough. It could never be enough. He moved his long, powerful hands down her frame and through the fabric of her cloak cupped the soft swell of her buttocks. On an agonized groan, he dragged her against the vee of his thighs.

Her head fell back and a long, keening moan whispered about them. "Will."

CHAPTER 10

CARA'S HOARSE ENTREATY WAS THE manner of breathy desire that had driven better men than William to their knees.

He ran his lips over her neck, gently grazing her skin with his teeth until he had wrung a gasp from her lips. "What hold do you have upon me?"

"Th-the same one y-you have upon m-me." Her breathless reply danced about him and he picked his head up. Her lips parted with desire, and her thick lashes hooding the passion teeming from her eyes hinted at a woman who'd welcome him between her thighs, and for one selfish instant, he ached with a physical hunger to be the first to lay claim to her innocence and not the bastard who would one day have the right to the delicate gift.

He slid his eyes closed, wanting to be one of those roguish sorts who'd put his own pleasure and hers before the honor of either of their names. Then, no truly honorable gentleman would be alone with an unwed lady, exploring her with his mouth, as he did now.

"Wh-why did you stop?" The tentative glimmer in her eyes wrenched at his heart.

William silently cursed and let his hands fall to his sides. "We can't do this, Cara." The muscles of his belly tightened. "You belong to another." Did those gravelly-spoken words dragged from his lungs belong to him? And though he was not betrothed by anything more than a pledge he'd given his father, his fate too was sealed. Ah, God, where once that truth had filled him with a gripping rage, now he wanted to rail at the fates for the loss of this woman. He'd sold his soul for merely eight years and this fleeting Christmastide meeting.

For a moment, pain contorted Cara's face and she may as well have thrust a dagger into his chest for the agony of causing her that hurt. "Well," she said, her voice small, at odds with that icy, unfeeling, clipped tone she'd adopted before.

Did she believe it did not matter to him that she'd one day belong to another? Some bloody, rotted bounder who'd be the first to lay her down and know the bliss of sliding into her innocent body. A red haze of jealousy stole across his vision, momentarily blinding him. It was safer that she believed him unaffected by the magic of these few days and yet he could not ride out with her not knowing she'd left an indelible mark upon his soul in ways he still could not right.

He tipped her chin up. "If circumstances were different," his lips pulled in a grimace and she slid her gaze down. "If I was a different man and you were a different lady and had we met…" before he'd taken that bloody barter. But then she would have been just a child. With that, an image danced forward of her as she would have been then. A young, lonely girl, alone with only her father's icy reserve for her guidance. Pain knifed at him. How he wished there had been someone for her all these years.

And how he wished to be that person now.

"It doesn't matter," she began, her gaze fixed on his neck.

William braced.

"It doesn't matter that you are illegitimate." Her words penetrated his earlier yearnings. He furrowed his brow. She believed he was a nobleman's by-blow? Even as he attempted to wrap his mind around the erroneous conclusion she'd drawn, Cara wet her lips. Emotion spilled from her eyes and threatened to suck him into the unspoken words hovering on her lips. Words he knew were coming. "I…" *Oh, God.* His gut clenched. For when she uttered them into existence, everything would change…and yet, nothing, all at the same rotted time. "I love you." *Oh, God.* Her words washed over him, scalding and freeing and enticing in ways he'd never known they could be.

"Oh, Cara mia." He brushed his lips over her temple.

"It doesn't matter," she said quickly and then her words ran over one another. "I know you likely believe it does to me because you think I am an ice princess without feelings." Shame sprang in his chest and spread through him. How unfairly he'd passed judgment. He'd not bothered to think that life had surely shaped her, just as he, too, had been shaped by his dream for freedom from the stifling life thrust upon him as a duke's son. Cara took his face between her palms. Even through the fabric of her damp gloves, her skin burned his. "I have spent years feeling nothing and believing myself incapable of feeling—anything—and not even wanting to." A half-laugh, half-sob bubbled past her bow-shaped lips. "But you saw that as a lie. You looked at me when no one before you has, not even my own family, and I want you." Her words echoed about the copse.

He closed his eyes once again with the promise she dangled before him—that dream his parents would withhold, for nothing more than a familial connection they'd forge with another. He opened and closed his mouth several times. Could he abandon the pledge he'd made his father? "We cannot." *But why can't I?* There was no formal contract. There was a promise made to his father and surely he'd free his son when William told him that he loved this woman.

The air froze in his chest.

I love her.

Cara's bell-like laughter rang in the clearing. "Of course we can. Don't you see?" She applied a gentle pressure to his cheeks. "I do not care what plans my father has for me or the man he'd have me wed. I want you."

And God help him... He pressed his eyes closed. He didn't care, either. That surely marked him dishonorable in so many ways, ways that mattered. But she mattered more. William looked at her again.

Her smile slipped. "D-do you not believe me?" Color suffused her cheeks. "Or do you think I cannot know these things after but a few days. I do, Will." She brushed her lips to his.

YEARS OF LADYLIKE DECORUM INGRAINED into Cara's every thought and actions screamed in protest, but she claimed control of her mind, and more, her feelings, thrilling at the power of it. The moment she had breathed her words of love for Will into truth, for the both of them, a giddy lightness had filled her chest. After Mother's passing, her father had sneered at her tears and loud grief for the loss of the woman who'd held her every night and every morning. How wrong he had been. There was nothing shameful in this. There was joy and beauty and a buoyant happiness that threatened to lift her up. How did she not see that before?

Because I did not know Will.

Cara ran her gaze over his cherished face and celebrated her ruin, not of revenge that her father would likely see any match between her and Will, but for the first time having control of her emotions.

She broke the kiss. "I love you," she whispered against his mouth. Her heart hung suspended to hear those precious words uttered back.

"I have not been fully truthful with you," he said at last, his tone gruff and hesitant in a way she'd not heard in any of their exchanges.

"Oh, God." Her heart dipped and then fell somewhere in her belly. A wave of coldness ran through her as an ugly, niggling possibility crept in. She sank back on her heels. Unwittingly, she scrabbled at her throat. "You *are* married." Her heart ripped open at the ugly possibility.

"No." The denial came from him harsh and guttural. He dragged a hand through his hair. "Do you think I would be here with you now if I was married?"

"I…" His words gave her pause. For that was precisely what she believed all men were capable of. Her father had proven himself a lecherous lord who took his pleasures where he willed it. The memories she had of her earlier years, when her mother lived, included a lonely woman weeping in her chambers when she'd not known her daughter listened in. It was from her mother she'd learned the cathartic healing that came from those wicked curse words. Will was different and even loving him as she did, she still didn't know what to make of it.

He cupped her neck. Running his fingers in a soothing back and forth rhythm, he caressed her nape. "You do not have much faith in the honor of a gentleman, do you?" Regret underscored his observation.

She mustered a wry smile. "I've not been given much reason to." Between her father, with his countless bastards littering the countryside, and her brother, who'd devoted his life to his own pleasures, she'd long ago accepted they were all self-serving fiends who'd place their own wants and desires above anyone and everyone.

And that was the world she'd be riding off into with the melting snow, no doubt, tomorrow. Unbidden, her gaze searched through the copse of trees to the stable where she'd left the earl's carriage. Panic churned in her belly. For when she made the journey from the Fox and Hare Inn, she'd forget to smile and laugh, and slowly become the cold, lonely ice princess hated by all.

She looked questioningly up at him. "What?"

"COME," WILLIAM SAID HARSHLY, AND shifted course, leading her deeper into the copse. He brought them to a halt beside a towering juniper. "Have you ever before made a Christmas bough, Cara?" he asked as he released her and walked beside the evergreen with its needle-like cones and blue berries.

From the corner of his eye, he detected the slight shake of her head. He bent and retrieved a dagger from his boot, then carefully set to work slicing off greenery the size of his hand. "Mistletoe was sacred to the Druids," he explained. "And once called *All Heal*. It was thought to bring good fortune and happiness." He held it up for her inspection and she tipped her head, studying it in silence. Then their eyes caught and held. "It was believed that no lady could refuse a kiss under the bough."

She touched the spindly needles with the tips of her fingers. "Oh, Will. You do not require a bough to secure my kiss." Despite the chill of the day, her cheeks burned at that boldness.

He dipped his head and captured her lips underneath his in a gentle meeting. Her hands fluttered between them and then she rested her delicate palms on his chest. His heart pounded. William lowered his brow to hers and drew in a deep breath. He'd thought this handful of days would be enough to sustain him through the cold future awaiting him. William could not honor the word he'd pledged his father years earlier. He could not walk away from Cara and the happiness she represented. William sucked in a breath, drawing in the mint and lemon scent so that it filled his senses. "I love you." She stilled. "And God help me, Cara, I cannot leave you." There was something beautifully freeing in uttering those words. The time for shame at breaking an oath he'd made to his parents would come later. But Cara represented forever.

She ran her gaze over him. Fear warred with hope. William ran his thumb along her lower lip. "I want you." But he wanted her in the way she deserved—to be properly courted, betrothed, and then ultimately married. Her lips parted and then a small sob escaped her. William folded his arms about her, drawing her against his chest. "I want to court you as you deserve. I don't care about the man who believes he has a claim to you," he said, rubbing his cheek over the silken softness of her curls.

Her body went still in his arms. "Oh, Will," she said brokenly. Cara drew back with pain burning in her eyes. "My father will never allow it."

He captured her hands in his and silenced her. She deserved the truth of his identity. "You asked for my story, Cara," he spoke in hushed tones. "I am not illegitimate."

She cocked her head.

"I am the heir to a dukedom."

Through the years, that revelation had been met with fawning and preening. Once more, Cara proved herself wholly unlike any other he'd known.

Her cheeks turned white to rival the unsullied snow upon the ground. Her hands went to her throat. "Wh-what?" He frowned as she took a faltering step away.

For the first time in the course of his twenty-six years, his birthright was met with whispered horror. Did she think he'd not wed her because of his title? He turned his palms up. "You asked if I was married…"

An agonized groan from Cara cut across his words and she staggered back, clamping her hands over her ears. "Oh, God, you *are* married." She stumbled over herself in her haste to be free of him and tumbled into the snow.

With a silent curse, William strode over to where she lay shivering in a drift, her expression stricken. He held a hand out and she flinched. Pointedly ignoring his offer of assistance, she shoved awkwardly to her feet. Of course, they'd known each other but these handful of days and, yet, her lack of faith in him spoke to her broken past and his pain that she'd believe him capable of that imagined infidelity. Even with the sting of the winter snow biting through the fabric of his pants, the hurt fury emanating from her taut frame threatened to spill over and burn him.

"No," he said hastily. He held a hand out, but she glared at his fingers. On a curse, he raked a hand through his hair. God, he was making a muck of this. "I am not unlike you. My father would see me wed to a woman whose familial connections he approves of." Cara hesitated and her rapidly drawn breaths filled the winter quiet. She peered at him with a narrow gaze and then some of the anger left her eyes. She still studied him with the same guardedness that could only come from the ugliness of her own existence as a pawn of a ruthless nobleman.

"Are you betrothed?" Her tone was flat; devoid of all emotion.

"No, Cara mia." He took her hands and, this time, she did not shove away his offering. "That is what I am trying to tell you. I was summoned by my father with the expectation that I'd wed her." His jaw tightened involuntarily at the young girl he remembered. "I knew her as nothing more than a child. She is my mother's god-daughter. My only memories of her were of a girl who was cold and cruel to her servants. I have spent the last eight years avoiding the responsibility expected of me." He gave his head a bitter shake.

"You do not love her, then?" she asked hesitantly.

He grimaced. "God, no." He raised her hands to his lips and brushed a kiss on the inside of each wrist. "She is the daughter of a duke, a miserable extension of her father."

Cara froze. "She is a duke's daughter?"

At the whispered words, William managed a brusque nod.

The color left Cara's cheeks. "Wh-what is her name, this m-miserable creature you'd not tie yourself to?"

He frowned at the shock radiating from the depths of her blue eyes. Did she believe he was a man who cared where titles were concerned? "Cara, it does not matter. There is no formal arrangement. There are no emotions engaged." He tipped her chin up. "I would marry you."

"What is her name?" she demanded, her tone shrill.

"Lady Clarisse Falcot, daughter of the Duke of Ravenscourt," he said quietly and, for one horrifying moment, he imagined she knew that woman.

However, if that name meant anything to her, she gave no indication. She simply slid her gaze off to a point beyond his shoulder. Her silence stood as the only response to his admission. After a long stretch of quiet punctuated by the shrill cry of a morning bird, Cara hugged her arms close to herself. "You would marry me," she said on a broken whisper. "But you do not truly know me." Bitterness and hurt made her words ragged. She rubbed her hands over her forearms. "You've known me but these few days and you knew that other woman how long? Eleven years?" She gave her head a slight shake. "Don't you see, I am that woman?"

William growled. "Do not say that," he commanded. He wrapped his arm about her forearm. "You are nothing like her."

"Aren't I?" She winged a regal, golden eyebrow upward. "I am the same woman who ordered a servant into a blizzard to obtain my baubles."

"It was your mother's necklace," he gritted out.

"And I'm the same woman who is cold and condescending."

How could she think she was anything like that woman his parents would see him wed? He opened his mouth, but then some sad glimmer in her fathomless, blue eyes spoke of a resignation. His breath stuck. By God, she'd reject him. For her words of love and the happiness she'd professed to know, she'd reject him. And for what? A misbegotten sense of who she was.

William proceeded slowly. One erroneously wrong word and he'd lose her forever. "At first, my opinion was such," he said quietly. "I have spent the past eight years avoiding any woman who reminds me of...of Lady Clarisse." His lips peeled back in an involuntary grimace at speaking the lady's name aloud. "I want you, Cara. I love you," he said with firmness in his tone, willing her to believe that truth.

CHAPTER 11

Lady Clarisse Falcot. Oh, God. The woman he'd spent years avoiding, was, in fact—her. Cara's stomach lurched. As Will spoke, his voice came as though down a long corridor.

Her muddied thoughts spun wildly, madly out of control. Will, her stranger in the inn, was none other than the man her father would betroth her to.

She stared at him as his lips moved, trying to make sense. There should be joy in knowing the man she'd fallen in love with was, in fact, her future betrothed. But there was not. There was a grim emptiness.

Tears popped behind Cara's eyelids and blurred Will's visage. A panicky half-sob, half-laugh stuck in her throat at the comedy of errors that was her life in this instance.

Since her mother's passing, all she'd wanted was to know love; wanted it, even as she'd known herself undeserving of that emotion. That wish to love and be loved had died a swift death at her father's hands. She'd learned early on her value and worth—and it had not been much. The pain of that, of knowing she mattered so very little to the man who'd given her life, had driven her to bury that need for love. To care for anyone was to know hurt and she didn't want any part of it.

Until Will. Until he'd shown her the splendor that came in feeling. And now this. The dream she'd carried deep within her heart, so very close, within her fingertips, and in her arms, and that dream was here. Yet, at the same time, she'd never been further from it.

She pressed her eyes closed and a single tear streaked down her cheek. This was to be her penance for the miserable, cruel creature she'd been. A woman who betrayed her half-sister, another victim of the duke's heartlessness. Another tear slipped behind the first. Followed by another and another.

"Oh, sweet Cara," Will whispered against her ear. He brushed his lips over her temple.

She cried because he'd spent eight years trying to forget her existence, just like everyone else. She cried because he deserved more than Lady Clarisse Falcot as his wife. "You must end it with," *me*. "h-her," her voice broke, and she cleared her throat. "Y-you must go to your f-father." The Duke of Billingsley, who'd smiled and laughed and whom she'd avoided when he'd come to visit because she didn't know what to make of such a very human duke. Oh, God. Another tear fell and she swiped it angrily away. "For the woman your father would have you wed, Will…she does not deserve you." He deserved a woman who was capable of light and laughter and goodness. She'd never been that woman and even the young man he'd been at eighteen had known it, early on and had wisely fled.

"Cara," he began quietly.

With fingers numb from the cold, she fished around the pocket sewn along the inside of her cloak. She withdrew the heart pendant and stared blankly down at the crimson ruby. For years, she'd tied love and happiness to this gift given long ago by her mother. Her throat muscles struggled to work. "I want you to have this," she said, pressing it into his hand. She wanted him to have it and remember the woman he'd met here who had been capable of feeling.

"I cannot," he protested, his tone gruff. He made to push it back into her hand, but she held her palms up.

"I want you to take it, Will. And I want you to remember how important it was for you to find a woman you loved and cared for. A woman who is not c-cruel." Her voice broke and she damned that slight catch, wanting to be done with this exchange, so she might climb in her carriage and return to the bleak, miserable existence she deserved.

Will pierced her with his blue-eyed stare. "I will come back for you."

She nodded. "I do not doubt you will." For that was the honorable, good man he was.

He brushed the pad of his glove-encased thumb over her lower lip. "Do you know, it occurs to me, love, that you've still not shared your identity?" The ghost of a smile played on his lips. "However am I to find you?"

You aren't. Oh, the time would inevitably come when their paths crossed and he knew that Lady Clarisse Falcot—cruel and cold—and Lady Cara, with no surname, were, in fact, one and the same. By then, hopefully he'd be married to one of those cheerful sorts, capable of warmth. *Oh, God.* She almost buckled under the pain of that.

Then a wry half-grin pulled his lips at the right corner. "As I intend to wed you, it seems only appropriate that I know the full name of the lady I will call my wife." Her heart squeezed at the boy-like quality of his smile. And with that expression of mirth, a memory slipped in of Will when she'd been just a girl of six. She'd been scolded by her father for resting her elbows on the table. He'd caught her eye across the table and winked once. Oh, God. It was too much. Agony twisted in her belly.

Some of the lightness dimmed in Will's eyes. "What is it?" he urged quietly.

She shook her head, incapable of words. "I-I am just…" Falling apart inside. "H-happy." She'd created such an effective mask these years; a façade she'd presented to Society, her family, and instructors and not once had anyone questioned the validity of her mask. Cara drew on years of practice in concealing emotion and flashed a sunny smile.

He kissed her; the faintest meeting of lips. "Cara mia?"

Determined to take this last moment with him, she twined her hands about his neck. "My name is Lady Cara Turner. My father is the Earl of Derby. I am journeying to his estate in L-Leeds," she stumbled over that mistruth. And fearing he'd see the lie in her eyes or hear it in her words, she kissed him.

Will froze against her and she moaned fearful he'd stop. For this was the last taste of passion she'd ever know. The thought of that truth sent panic spiraling through her. She kissed him hard and he parted her mouth with his lips. He slid his tongue inside and found hers so that they mated in a primitive dance that should have shocked her as a proper lady but instead only resulted in a wet heat at her core.

Will clasped her buttocks and dragged her closer. She moaned, wanting more of him. Wanting all of him.

That jerked her to the moment. Her chest rose and fell with the rapidity of her breath. She passed her gaze over the precious lines of his sculpted cheeks, the noble jaw, the slight dimple in his right cheek. He eyed her through those thick lashes no man had a right to possess. "I love you, Will." And she would forever love him for all the gifts he'd given her. None of them of the material sort, but more precious for what they'd shown her about herself.

"I love you, Cara." The wind shook the branches overhead and sent snow tumbling into the drift in a noiseless fall.

If he utters those words once more, I will be lost. I will be the selfish, self-centered creature I've always been.

"Cara, I—"

"We should return." Unable to meet the piercing intensity of his gaze, she glanced past his shoulder. "My maid will be missing me."

Will shot a hand around her forearm, staying her retreat. "I *will* come for you," he said with a quiet insistence. Concern radiated from his intelligent eyes.

Ah, through her false smile and feigned happiness, he'd seen the underlying agony taking apart what was left of her. Then, he'd been the only person to truly look at her.

His first judgment had been the correct one. "I know."

Wordlessly, they made their way back to the miserable, little inn.

And that afternoon when Will rode off to break a pledge he'd made to his father, Cara boarded her borrowed carriage once more and left the only place she'd ever been truly happy.

CHAPTER 12

WILLIAM TOOK IN THE FAMILIAR halls, corridors he'd raced wildly down as a child, driving his tutors and nursemaids to near madness. Evergreen boughs with holly berries and apples hung along the walls. He pressed his palm against the front of his jacket pocket. The makeshift bough he'd collected alongside Cara that morning, resonated heat in his pocket.

With each step, his muddied boots trailed moisture and dirt on the sapphire blue carpet. His father's butler, a young man with a serious set to his face at some point had replaced the old, grinning Halpert, shot a frown over his shoulder. At the very least, he should have changed his attire before storming into the Billingsley household as though he'd not been gone almost eight years; more a guest who came to call periodically. They stopped beside his father's office door. And yet, he'd little intention of remaining. There was someone he longed to see more.

The butler rapped once and then tossed the door open. In his drawn out, nasal tones, the man announced William. "Lord Grafton."

The Duke of Billingsley sat on the leather button sofa over by the hearth, his wife curled at his side in a bucolic tableau that defied the norms of most *ton* marriages. His parents stared, frozen, wearing the look of two who'd seen a ghost.

"Mother, Father," he greeted, dusting his palms along the sides of his breeches.

The servant backed out of the room and his departure sprang his parents to action. With a cry, his mother climbed to her feet and raced across the room in a manner that would raise the brows of polite Society. Then, wrong or right, there were certain liberties permitted a duchess. "William," she rasped and flung her arms about him, holding tight.

He folded her in his arms. "Mother," he repeated, his throat thick with emotion. He'd not regretted the years he'd spent traveling, but there was a staggering shock in finding how time had marched on, aging his parents in his absence.

How he'd missed them. His absence, however, had been of his choosing.

On the heel of that were thoughts of Cara as she'd been since her mother's passing; alone, without anyone to love or care for her—through no choice of her own.

"Oh, William," his mother wept against his chest. He patted her back.

Would she feel this same overwhelming emotion when, after eight years, he asked to be pardoned of the responsibility to wed her goddaughter? William stiffened as the ugly, niggling reminder of what he'd ask this day surged forward. "Father," he said cautiously to the bear of a man eying him from over by the hearth.

The duke stood with his hands clasped behind his back, an indecipherable look in his eyes that may as well have belonged to his son. Determined to have out with it, William spoke.

"There is a matter I would speak with you about."

"What is it, William?" With only a mother's intuitiveness, the duchess stepped away and William made his way over to where his father remained rooted to the floor.

He held a hand out, but his father only enfolded it in his equally large fingers and pulled him close. "My boy," he whispered and hugged him with a ferocity that momentarily cut off airflow.

Where William had come and gone through the years, flitting about the Continent and countries, there was a permanency to this homecoming. For the joy of this moment, for the love he knew from his parents, there was a gripping pain for Cara—forgotten at Christmas, alone in an inn without so much as a brother or father who remembered her existence. His throat closed and he stepped away from his father.

His father dropped his eyebrows. "What is it?" he said gruffly.

His mother looked back and forth between them.

He'd had hours to prepare for this exchange. In all he'd run through in his mind, nothing seemed adequate for what he'd put to his parents. Never one to prevaricate, William drew in a steadying breath. "I met a woman," he said, meeting his father's gaze.

The older man puzzled his brow. "A woman?"

For all the perplexity to that question, William may as well have just stated his intentions to climb astride Perseus' mythical horse and take flight. "I had every intention of seeing to my responsibilities and wedding Lady Clarisse," he continued quietly.

His father snapped his eyebrows together in an angry line. "And?" That single syllable utterance rumbled off the walls.

"On my journey home, I was…" *captivated by a spirited lady and could not bring myself to leave.*

His father gave him a probing look. "William?"

William cleared his throat. "Forgive me," he said, finishing his previous thought. "I was delayed by the snow. I took shelter at an inn." Had it only been three days? The joy he'd known in those three days outweighed every single one of the eight years he'd been gone. "And while I was there, I met her."

"Met who?" His father glowered in the show of anger William had expected.

"I do not understand, William." His mother spoke with a slowness of one trying to muddle her way through a conundrum.

"I met a young lady. Lady Cara Turner, the Earl of Derby's daughter," he said quietly, ignoring the shocked confusion in his mother's eyes. An image of Cara as she'd been with his face clasped between her delicate fingers flashed to his mind. He reached into the front of his pocket and withdrew the crimson heart she'd given him. That last link she'd had to her mother, she'd entrusted with him. He gripped the precious gift. "And I fell in love with her." He held his father's hard stare. "I had every intention of honoring my pledge to you, but not any longer. I cannot marry Lady Clarisse."

Silence met his admission. William braced for his father's booming fury but his mother shattered the quiet, interrupting whatever words were on her husband's lips. "Did you say the Earl of Derby's daughter, Lady Nora?"

He shook his head. "Lady Cara."

His mother gave him a gentle look. "But William, the earl's only daughter is Lady Nora."

William must have heard his mother's words wrong. A buzzing filled his ears and he gave his head a clearing shake. "You are mistaken." His words came as though down a corridor.

The duke folded his arms at his chest and snorted. "Your mother isn't wrong on any matters of the *ton*."

She nodded in agreement. "He is correct, I am invariably right on all these matters."

William tried to make sense of her confounding words. Why would Cara lie to him about her identity? The air left him on a shuddery hiss. And how in blazes was he to find her if she'd given him a false name? He shook his head hard, dispelling the doubts planted by his mother. "You are wrong," he snapped. Cara wouldn't have deceived him. His insides twisted in an agonizing grip. Why would she? It did not make sense.

"I am not." His mother wrinkled her nose. "Well, at least not about the earl having a daughter named Nora and *not* having a daughter named *Cara*."

"You are certain?" he demanded.

The duchess gave a hesitant nod.

William scrubbed one hand down his face and, with a panicked energy running through him, spun on his heel and began to pace. "Is this a ploy to make me abandon my intentions to wed the lady?"

That shameful question had wrung gasps from his parents. "William," his mother chided.

He increased his frantic movements. Nothing else made sense. Why would Cara have given him a false name? Why—? He stopped abruptly and stared at the crimson heart in his gloved palm. Pain stabbed at his belly. He shook his head. "She would not lie." She would not have given him this gift and let him ride off, knowing they'd never again meet. William closed his eyes hard and fought to make semblance of what his mother was saying.

"How did you come by Clarisse's pendant?"

His mother's quietly spoken question brought his eyes open. He stared numbly on as his mother came closer. She bowed her head over the ruby necklace in his palm and he folded his hand closed.

Sharing this part of Cara seemed... Then his mother's words registered. "What?" He opened his hand. "This is Cara's." No! It was impossible.

"No," his mother said gently, slipping the broken pendant from his grip. She turned it over in her hands. "This belonged to Cynthia." Her closest friend who'd died... His mind shuttered. Oh, God, it could not be. His mother peeled her lip back in a snarl, her eyes flashing a hatred he'd not believed her capable of. "Her husband forbid her from wearing—"

"Anything but diamonds," the words left him on a slow exhale.

She nodded slowly. "Yes, yes, that is correct. How do you—?" His mother widened her eyes in shock. "It is her. *She* is your Cara."

Cara mia.

"I don't understand," his father boomed.

Neither did he. William's mind spun. The woman he'd spent years running from was now the only woman he wanted or needed. *She was cold and cruel to her servants and devoid of all feeling...and I have spent the last eight years avoiding the responsibility expected of me.* His stomach churned with nausea as he went over every last, rotted word he'd uttered to her.

Don't you see, I am that woman...?

Bile climbed up his throat until he thought he'd be sick. She'd been telling him with even her words, her identity, and he'd been so consumed by age-old resentments over a vow his father had expected of him, that he'd failed to see that which was truly before his eyes.

His throat muscles worked. "What a bloody fool I've been," he breathed. In sending him away, she'd set him free. He closed his eyes. How could she not know he was only free when she was in his life? And he'd left her. Alone, at the blasted inn.

"Wh-where is she?" his mother put forth with the same unease cloying at his thoughts.

He attempted to right his tumultuous thoughts. Where would she go? Off to that miserable bastard who'd sired her; the only good he'd done in the whole of his loathsome life? Then understanding dawned. William spun on his heel and stalked off.

"William," his father thundered. "Where are you going?"

He squared his jaw. "To collect my betrothed." And when he did, he intended to spend the rest of his life filling her days with joy and making atonement for being such an odious beast.

CHAPTER 13

THESE WERE SORRY DAYS INDEED when a lady willingly chose to spend Christmas at Mrs. Belden's miserable halls.

Properly attired in her ivory satin gown, Cara lay on her side, her breath frozen. Once again, she stared at walls but altogether different ones than the thin, whitewashed panels of the Fox and Hare Inn. This room sterile, yet perfect. There was no water stained ceilings or cold winter breezes stealing through the window. She flipped onto her back and flung her arm across her brow. A sad smile pulled at her lips. She'd have traded all of her father's properties gladly for the possession of that miserable, little inn. There had been more beauty and happiness in that aged establishment than in any place she'd had the misfortune of calling home in any of her eighteen years.

In one great twist of irony, she'd almost had every happiness she never believed herself deserving of, or even possible... Her throat worked. Will was *her* William. That man she'd despised all these years for being a future duke and emotionless nobleman her father would wed her to. She caught her lower lip hard. He'd never been any of those things she'd silently accused him of being, whereas she? She had been the very cruel, cold, and calculated person he'd taken her as. And for that, she'd freed him.

A shuddery sob spilled past her lips. She rolled onto her side again and hugged her arms tight about herself. Her skin still burned with the feel of another pair of arms folded about her. True to the selfish, needy lady she'd been for the course of her life, she wanted more of him. Wanted all of him. She swiped a hand over her face. "Enough," she whispered. Cara shoved herself up and swung her legs over the edge of the bed. The mattress groaned with the slight depression of her weight. The sunlight filtered through the open curtains and she squinted at the stream of light as it drew her back to another sunny day inside a copse of juniper trees. For all the agony of losing him, happiness danced within her heart at the fleeting joy she'd known.

A knock sounded at the door. "My lady?" Alison's happy voice sounded from the other side of the door.

Cara cast a glance over her shoulder and her lips twisted in a wry smile. Ah, the summons. One week too late. Or mayhap, just in time. Had her father's carriage arrived when it ought, she'd have traveled on to his miserable, cold, and lonely estate. She would still be the same shallow, selfish creature who shut out the thoughts and feelings of others and protected herself. She gripped the edge of her bed. Mayhap this was the one gift her father had given her.

Another rap. "My lady? You have been summoned below."

Of course the summons was due. Her father would invariably remember he had a daughter somewhere when he had use of her. Did he even now realize that the long-standing arrangement between him and the Duke of Billingsley binding their children had been severed? There could never be triumph in thwarting her father's wishes when it had also shattered her heart.

"My lady?" Some of Alison's usual cheer faded to a cautious concern.

With a sigh, she came to her feet. "Just a moment, Alison." She made her way across the room, pausing beside her vanity. A miserable creature with red eyes and wan cheeks stared back at her. Cara attempted to pinch some color into her pale skin. Her eyes remained rimmed with red, a testament to her tears. Abandoning all futile efforts to be the cool, unaffected lady she'd been before William, she made her way to the door and pulled it open.

Alison smiled. "You are…" Her happiness dimmed as she took in Cara's face. Her gaze lingered on Cara's cheeks. "You have been summoned to the Green Parlor, my lady."

So her father had managed to remember her, at last.

"Thank you," she replied. Except, by the flare of shock in Alison's eyes, it only served to remind Cara once more of a nobleman who was kind to all, regardless of station or lot in life. A man so very different than her father—or her. Averting her eyes so her maid could not see the blasted sheen of tears misting her vision. "Alison, will you see that I'm all ready to depart?" Again.

The girl nodded and rushed into the room.

Cara continued down the corridor, her footsteps echoed off the corridor walls. How very sadly similar this day was to another not even a week prior. Only, no laughter chimed from the rooms of other students or excited prattling filled the corridors of young women excited to return home for the holiday season. She'd been so very condescending to her fellow students; mocking their happiness, jeering their love of the inanity. She winced. What a foul creature she'd been. Cara paused at the edge of the Green Parlor and layered her back against the ivory damask wallpaper.

"You deserve more...You deserve to love and be loved. You deserve to laugh and know there is no shame in feeling..."

She caught her lip hard as desperate fear pounded at her breast; the sickening possibility that once the warm memory of William faded, and she returned home, with the inevitable prospect of making a match with some other lord her father approved of. Cara stared angrily at the opposite wall and balled her fists. She did not want hurt and resentment to transform her into the cold, hateful creature she'd been. "I will not be that woman," she mouthed.

No. She would not be manipulated as a pawn on her father's chessboard of power. She'd not wed any gentleman just because her loathsome sire ordained the match. Cara froze, as a giddy fluttering danced about her belly. Since her mother's death she'd been groomed and coached by the most distinguished instructors in the kingdom; molded into a shell of a person Society approved of. That control she'd turned naively over, unwillingly as a child. A slow, triumphant smile that would have appalled her father, should he see it, turned her lips up in a wide grin. Too long she'd given her happiness over to others. William had shown her there was no shame in a lady feeling. As such, she'd never have him, but she would have some control of her life.

Squaring her shoulders, she took a step, and then stopped. A small kissing bough made of juniper cones hung at the center of the doorway. Cara blinked. Her heart thumped loudly in her ears as she recalled a different juniper and then her skin burned hot with awareness and she slowly lowered her gaze. Then the rapidly pounding organ in her chest ceased to beat altogether.

Arms clasped at his back, William stood in the center of the parlor. Except… Cara tipped her head. The elegantly clad gentleman in his midnight claw hammer coat and buckskin breeches bore no hint of the rough stranger in coarse Holland cotton breeches and a rough cap. "Clarisse." His gruff baritone washed over her like the warmth of a summer sun's rays.

She slid her eyes closed and allowed the husky sound to envelope her in a soft caress. Then his greeting registered. Her eyes shot open. Not Cara. *Clarisse.* She smoothed her palms over her skirts. "Y-you called me Clarisse," she said taking a step away. Of course, he would eventually discover the identity of the lady he'd thrown snowballs with outside the Fox and Hare Inn. She'd just not expected it would be but two days later. She continued her retreat.

William dropped his arms to his sides. He sent one chestnut eyebrow winging up. "Is that not your name?"

"It is." Her back knocked against the wall and she gave thanks for the support that kept her upright, even as her legs went weak at the confusion of William's presence here. Now. She cast a glance about, wetting her lips. Surely the proper Mrs. Belden would never permit this unchaperoned meeting between a duke's daughter and an unmarried gentleman.

"I explained we were betrothed," he said quietly, correctly interpreting the path her thoughts had wandered. He folded his arms before him. "Did you think you'd leave that inn and I'd not ever find out the identity of the woman who threw my world off-kilter?"

Oh, God. Agony wrenched her heart. What game did he play? "W-we are not betrothed." She despised the breathlessly weak quality of her rebuttal.

Through narrowed eyes, he watched her retreat. "Ah, but we almost were," he said tormenting her with that softly spoken statement. And this time, with his long, graceful strides he ate away the distance between them.

Cara remained fixed to her spot. She'd spent almost the whole of her life retreating—from pain, from strangers, and herself. Cara pressed her hands to the wall borrowing artificial support from the cold, hard plaster. "How did you find…" She allowed her words to trail off.

He gave her a droll smile. "How did I learn you'd given Lady Nora's identity as your own?"

Guilt twisted at that lie. Even if it had been a deception to set him free, it spoke to her honor. Cara managed a nod.

William reached into his pocket and she studied his slow, precise movements as he withdrew a familiar necklace. Her throat closed as he held up the shimmering, crimson ruby she'd never separated from—until now. Until him. "Imagine my parents' shock when I went to them asking to be freed of my obligations to Lady Clarisse Falcot, because I'd lost my heart quite desperately to another woman." He looked from the necklace in his large palm to her. "Only for my mother to question just how I'd come by your mother's necklace. I would have come yesterday so you did not wake up alone." Again. "On this Christmas day." He let the gold chain dangle between his fingers and the shimmering ruby twisted and danced. "But I had your chain repaired first. You lost it before, Cara." He took a step toward her. "I will not have it lost again."

She sought to decipher some of what he was feeling in his smooth, modulated tone. Was he angry? Embarrassed? His face may as well have been set into an unyielding mask. "Why are you here?" she pleaded.

She stiffened as he shot out his other hand and then slowly, in a hypnotic, gentle motion ran his knuckles over her jaw. "How could I not come for you, Clarisse?"

Emotion clogged her throat. Why was he doing this? "Do not call me that." Her words came out as a ragged entreaty. "I despise that name." Chosen by her father, she hated it for that alone.

William flicked his gaze over her face, his eyes lingering on hers. Pain sparked in their blue depths, but then was quickly gone. Did he see the evidence of the tears she'd cried for him? Once, that weakness would have shamed her. No longer. Because of him. He'd taught her there was no shame in one's tears or hurts.

"Very well," he said quietly. "Cara." His use of her name, the only soul other than her mother who'd uttered it and with such tenderness, gutted her. He'd been clear in his hopes for his future and that hope had not been a cruel, unkind lady who'd sneered at servants and shamed her own half-sister. "Why did you not tell me?" he demanded, his tone harsher than she'd ever remembered, even from that day of their first meeting.

Filled with a restiveness, she ducked around his arm and rushed away. "What would you have me say?" she rasped. "That I was the very same woman you spent years avoiding?" He flinched. "And with good reason." She'd not allow him that silent guilt. Jaw quivering, she angled it up. "You were correct in all your suppositions about me, William." There'd been very little redeeming about her as a person.

"I was wrong." Emotion roughened his tone. "I love you."

Her heart soared, as his words lifted her, in ways she'd not been since their stolen moments at the Fox and Hare Inn, but then it swiftly fell back into place. "You do not truly know me," she said softly. He'd been more accurate in his first impressions, when he'd correctly gauged the ugly inside her. Cara gave her head a little shake. "Not after three days. The girl you remember, the one who ordered her servants about and was incapable of warmth and kindness, that is who I've been longer and you deserve more than that."

Anger emanated from his frame as he stalked over and took her by the shoulders. The ruby heart pendant he held in his hand burned through the fabric of her gown. "Do not presume to tell me what I deserve or desire. I want you, Cara." He gentled his grip and drew her close. "I love *you*." His words emerged with the strength and resolve better suited to conquerors of old.

Cara wrenched away from him. "Do you know the type of person I am?" she cried.

He swept his lashes down, silently urging her to continue.

She backed up several steps, putting distance between them. "I-I am the kind of woman who had her half-sister sacked because the sight of her reminded me of my despicable father and his inability to love me."

He stilled and, coward that she was, Cara slid her gaze over to the bright-burning hearth in the corner, unable to confront the evidence of his disgust. "I have no friends because I'm unkind and cold." Just as he'd said. Tears blurred her eyes and she blinked them back.

Large hands settled on her shoulders, startling her. She'd not heard his quiet approach. Then, the familiar weight of a gold chain settled about her neck and a spark of warmth singed her skin at the reunion. With shaking fingers, she touched her mother's pendant that Will had fastened about her. He turned her about to face him. "You are no longer that woman."

Her soul clung to the sliver of hope that he was indeed correct; a tantalizing possibility that would free her of the chains of this horrid creature she'd been for eleven years. "But what if I am?" she whispered. What if that vileness was in her blood and could not be forever buried because it was an inextricable part of her soul?

"Oh, Cara, the very fact that you worry as much means you are not that woman." William raised her knuckles to his mouth, kissing first one hand, then the other. "You crafted such a perfect façade for the world of a remote ice princess that even you believed it. I saw past that to the woman who smiled and cursed." His lips twitched. "And who wished to be kind and know kindness." He brushed his lips over hers in a faint meeting. "Marry me."

For a moment she believed the whisper, part of the dream she'd carried from the Fox and Hare Inn, echoing around her mind. She tried to drag forth breath to make words, but had nothing. Cara shook her head.

He grinned, the half-smile that dimpled his cheek and gave him a boyish look. "Is that a no?"

"I—" *Am not that person.* The lady her father and Society had spent years shaping, had been a hollow, empty figure of the woman she was, and more, the woman she was learning to be. She smiled gently up at William. "That is a yes." A single tear squeezed past her lashes and slid down her cheek.

William widened his smile and then, lowering his head, claimed her mouth.

Cara returned his kiss and for the first time in eleven years, she knew love.

EPILOGUE

London, England
January, 1818

⁋IN THE QUIET, EMPTY STREETS of London, the carriage sat outside the townhouse, as it had for…well, Cara knew not how long, but at the very least, knew it had been a good deal of time. Not that it mattered *how* much time had passed. There were more important matters to attend. She peeled the curtain back ever so faintly and peaked out the window then gulped and let it fall promptly into place.

"Er, you do realize we've been sitting here for almost fifteen minutes, love?"

"Hmm?" She swung her attention up to her husband who occupied the seat beside her on the bench. He was saying something. What was he saying? She tried to order her muddled thoughts. Cara swallowed hard and stole another look outside at the front façade of the Marquess of Waverly's townhouse. Anxiety roiled through her. Then, it was not every day a lady went to make amends with the half-sister she'd so wronged in life. William settled his hand over hers and she took undeserved strength from that offering. "She hates me."

"Perhaps," he said with an honest directness she appreciated. "But you will hate yourself more if you do not attempt to make amends."

Cara caught her lower lip and stared at the red velvet curtain covering the carriage window. Yes, her husband was indeed, correct. If she did not meet her sister and ask for her pardon, she'd not forgive herself, and yet… This was about something so much more than her own eased conscience.

This was about…two sisters who'd been shaped by their own experiences as the Duke of Ravenscourt's unfortunate daughters, a bond that no one but those wronged children might understand. The woman she'd been at one time would have scoffed at the very idea of asking forgiveness of a woman who, through her efforts, had lost her position. But William was correct. She'd been changed. By him. By their time at the Fox and Hare Inn. And more, because love had flooded her life.

Aware of her husband's gaze on her, she gave a slight nod and then drew in a breath. "It is time," she said softly.

He quickly rapped on the carriage door and the driver pulled it open.

Her husband leapt to the ground and then held a hand up to assist her down. Cara's gaze crept up the length of the townhouse and unease churned within her. *What if she does not wish to see me?* Then, why should she wish to? As all the doubts and indecision paraded through her mind, the wind pulled at her cloak. She touched the pendant about her neck for strength. "I am ready."

William slid his fingers into hers and gave her hand a slight, reassuring squeeze. They reached the front door of the marquess' townhouse and as though he feared she'd change her mind, William knocked once.

"What if she does not wish to see me?" the question slipped from her lips, followed by a stream of inquiries she could not hold back. "What if she has words of hate and loathing? What if she tells me she doesn't care to ever speak to me again?"

"Then you will know." He applied gentle pressure to her fingers once more. "I am here, Cara mia. You aren't alone."

With the surety of his love, her fear receded and she gave a nod. Cara let her breath out on a slow exhale as her unease faded. "I am ready," she said softly. "As long as you are beside me."

William raised her knuckles to his lips. "Always," he pledged. "I will always be beside you."

Cara smiled up at him.

For the first time, she was not alone.

THE END

OTHER BOOKS BY CHRISTI CALDWELL

TO ENCHANT A WICKED DUKE
Book 13 in the "Heart of a Duke" Series by Christi Caldwell

A Devil in Disguise

Years ago, when Nick Tallings, the recent Duke of Huntly, watched his family destroyed at the hands of a merciless nobleman, he vowed revenge. But his efforts had been futile, as his enemy, Lord Rutland is without weakness.

Until now…

With his rival finally happily married, Nick is able to set his ruthless scheme into motion. His plot hinges upon Lord Rutland's innocent, empty-headed sister-in-law, Justina Barrett. Nick will ruin her, marry her, and then leave her brokenhearted.

A Lady Dreaming of Love

From the moment Justina Barrett makes her Come Out, she is labeled a Diamond. Even with her ruthless father determined to sell her off to the highest bidder, Justina never gives up on her hope for a good, honorable gentleman who values her wit more than her looks.

A Not-So-Chance Meeting

Nick's ploy to ensnare Justina falls neatly into place in the streets of London. With each carefully orchestrated encounter, he slips further and further inside the lady's heart, never anticipating that Justina, with her quick wit and strength, will break down his own defenses. As Nick's plans begins to unravel, he's left to determine which is more important—Justina's love or his vow for vengeance. But can Justina ever forgive the duke who deceived her?

ONE WINTER WITH A BARON
Book 12 in the "Heart of a Duke" Series by Christi Caldwell

A clever spinster:

Content with her spinster lifestyle, Miss Sybil Cunning wants to prove that a future as an unmarried woman is the only life for her. As a bluestocking who values hard, empirical data, Sybil needs help with her research. Nolan Pratt, Baron Webb, one of society's most scandalous rakes, is the perfect gentleman to help her. After all, he inspires fear in proper mothers and desire within their daughters.

A notorious rake:

Society may be aware of Nolan Pratt, Baron's Webb's wicked ways, but what he has carefully hidden is his miserable handling of his family's finances. When Sybil presents him the opportunity to earn much-needed funds, he can't refuse.

A winter to remember:

However, what begins as a business arrangement becomes something more and with every meeting, Sybil slips inside his heart. Can this clever woman look beneath the veneer of a coldhearted rake to see the man Nolan truly is?

TO REDEEM A RAKE
Book 11 in the "Heart of a Duke" Series by Christi Caldwell

He's spent years scandalizing society.
Now, this rake must change his ways.

Society's most infamous scoundrel, Daniel Winterbourne, the Earl of Montfort, has been promised a small fortune if he can relinquish his wayward, carousing lifestyle. And behaving means he must also help find a respectable companion for his youngest sister—someone who will guide her and whom she can emulate. However, Daniel knows no such woman. But when he encounters a childhood friend, Daniel believes she may just be the answer to all of his problems.

Having been secretly humiliated by an unscrupulous blackguard years earlier, Miss Daphne Smith dreams of finding work at Ladies of Hope, an institution that provides an education for disabled women. With her sordid past and a disfigured leg, few opportunities arise for a woman such as she. Knowing Daniel's history, she wishes to avoid him, but working for his sister is exactly the stepping stone she needs.

Their attraction intensifies as Daniel and Daphne grow closer, preparing his sister for the London Season. But Daniel must resist his desire for a woman tarnished by scandal while Daphne is reminded of the boy she once knew. Can society's most notorious rake redeem his reputation and become the man Daphne deserves?

To Woo a Widow

Book 10 in the "Heart of a Duke" Series by Christi Caldwell

They see a brokenhearted widow.
She's far from shattered.

Lady Philippa Winston is never marrying again. After her late husband's cruelty that she kept so well hidden, she has no desire to search for love.

Years ago, Miles Brookfield, the Marquess of Guilford, made a frivolous vow he never thought would come to fruition—he promised to marry his mother's goddaughter if he was unwed by the age of thirty. Now, to his dismay, he's faced with honoring that pledge. But when he encounters the beautiful and intriguing Lady Philippa, Miles knows his true path in life. It's up to him to break down every belief Philippa carries about gentlemen, proving that not only is love real, but that he is the man deserving of her sheltered heart.

Will Philippa let down her guard and allow Miles to woo a widow in desperate need of his love?

The Lure of a Rake
Book 9 in the "Heart of a Duke" Series by Christi Caldwell

A Lady Dreaming of Love

Lady Genevieve Farendale has a scandalous past. Jilted at the altar years earlier and exiled by her family, she's now returned to London to prove she can be a proper lady. Even though she's not given up on the hope of marrying for love, she's wary of trusting again. Then she meets Cedric Falcot, the Marquess of St. Albans whose seductive ways set her heart aflutter. But with her sordid history, Genevieve knows a rake can also easily destroy her.

An Unlikely Pairing

What begins as a chance encounter between Cedric and Genevieve becomes something more. As they continue to meet, passions stir. But with Genevieve's hope for true love, she fears Cedric will be unable to give up his wayward lifestyle. After all, Cedric has spent years protecting his heart, and keeping everyone out. Slowly, she chips away at all the walls he's built, but when he falters, Genevieve can't offer him redemption. Now, it's up to Cedric to prove to Genevieve that the love of a man is far more powerful than the lure of a rake.

To Trust a Rogue
Book 8 in the "Heart of a Duke" Series by Christi Caldwell

A rogue

Marcus, the Viscount Wessex has carefully crafted the image of rogue and charmer for Polite Society. Under that façade, however, dwells a man whose dreams were shattered almost eight years earlier by a young lady who captured his heart, pledged her love, and then left him, with nothing more than a curt note.

A widow

Eight years earlier, faced with no other choice, Mrs. Eleanor Collins, fled London and the only man she ever loved, Marcus, Viscount Wessex. She has now returned to serve as a companion for her elderly aunt with a daughter in tow. Even though they're next door neighbors, there is little reason for her to move in the same circles as Marcus, just in case, she vows to avoid him, for he reminds her of all she lost when she left.

Reunited

As their paths continue to cross, Marcus finds his desire for Eleanor just as strong, but he learned long ago she's not to be trusted. He will offer her a place in his bed, but not anything more. Only, Eleanor has no interest in this new, roguish man. The more time they spend together, the protective wall they've constructed to keep the other out, begin to break. With all the betrayals and secrets between them, Marcus has to open his heart again. And Eleanor must decide if it's ever safe to trust a rogue.

To Wed His Christmas Lady
Book 7 in the "Heart of a Duke" Series by Christi Caldwell

She's longing to be loved:

Lady Cara Falcot has only served one purpose to her loathsome father—to increase his power through a marriage to the future Duke of Billingsley. As such, she's built protective walls about her heart, and presents an icy facade to the world around her. Journeying home from her finishing school for the Christmas holidays, Cara's carriage is stranded during a winter storm. She's forced to tarry at a ramshackle inn, where she immediately antagonizes another patron—William.

He's avoiding his duty in favor of one last adventure:

William Hargrove, the Marquess of Grafton has wanted only one thing in life—to avoid the future match his parents would have him make to a cold, duke's daughter. He's returning home from a blissful eight years of traveling the world to see to his responsibilities. But when a winter storm interrupts his trip and lands him at a falling-down inn, he's forced to share company with a commanding Lady Cara who initially reminds him exactly of the woman he so desperately wants to avoid.

A Christmas snowstorm ushers in the spirit of the season:

At the holiday time, these two people who despise each other due to first perceptions are offered renewed beginnings and fresh starts. As this gruff stranger breaks down the walls she's built about herself, Cara has to determine whether she can truly open her heart to trusting that any man is capable of good and that she herself is capable of love. And William has to set aside all previous thoughts he's carried of the polished ladies like Cara, to be the man to show her that love.

THE HEART OF A SCOUNDREL
Book 6 in the "Heart of a Duke" Series by Christi Caldwell

Ruthless, wicked, and dark, the Marquess of Rutland rouses terror in the breast of ladies and nobleman alike. All Edmund wants in life is power. After he was publically humiliated by his one love Lady Margaret, he vowed vengeance, using Margaret's niece, as his pawn. Except, he's thwarted by another, more enticing target— Miss Phoebe Barrett.

Miss Phoebe Barrett knows precisely the shame she's been born to. Because her father is a shocking letch she's learned to form her own opinions on a person's worth. After a chance meeting with the Marquess of Rutland, she is captivated by the mysterious man. He, too, is a victim of society's scorn, but the more encounters she has with Edmund, the more she knows there is powerful depth and emotion to the jaded marquess.

The lady wreaks havoc on Edmund's plans for revenge and he finds he wants Phoebe, at all costs. As she's drawn into the darkness of his world, Phoebe risks being destroyed by Edmund's ruthlessness. And Phoebe who desires love at all costs, has to determine if she can ever truly trust the heart of a scoundrel.

To Love a Lord
Book 5 in the "Heart of a Duke" Series by Christi Caldwell

All she wants is security:

The last place finishing school instructor Mrs. Jane Munroe belongs, is in polite Society. Vowing to never wed, she's been scuttled around from post to post. Now she finds herself in the Marquess of Waverly's household. She's never met a nobleman she liked, and when she meets the pompous, arrogant marquess, she remembers why. But soon, she discovers Gabriel is unlike any gentleman she's ever known.

All he wants is a companion for his sister:

What Gabriel finds himself with instead, is a fiery spirited, bespectacled woman who entices him at every corner and challenges his age-old vow to never trust his heart to a woman. But... there is something suspicious about his sister's companion. And he is determined to find out just what it is.

All they need is each other:

As Gabriel and Jane confront the truth of their feelings, the lies and secrets between them begin to unravel. And Jane is left to decide whether or not it is ever truly safe to love a lord.

Loved By a Duke
Book 4 in the "Heart of a Duke" Series by Christi Caldwell

For ten years, Lady Daisy Meadows has been in love with Auric, the Duke of Crawford. Ever since his gallant rescue years earlier, Daisy knew she was destined to be his Duchess. Unfortunately, Auric sees her as his best friend's sister and nothing more. But perhaps, if she can manage to find the fabled heart of a duke pendant, she will win over the heart of her duke.

Auric, the Duke of Crawford enjoys Daisy's company. The last thing he is interested in however, is pursuing a romance with a woman he's known since she was in leading strings. This season, Daisy is turning up in the oddest places and he cannot help but notice that she is no longer a girl. But Auric wouldn't do something as foolhardy as to fall in love with Daisy. He couldn't. Not with the guilt he carries over his past sins… Not when he has no right to her heart…But perhaps, just perhaps, she can forgive the past and trust that he'd forever cherish her heart—but will she let him?

THE LOVE OF A ROGUE
Book 3 in the "Heart of a Duke" Series by Christi Caldwell

Lady Imogen Moore hasn't had an easy time of it since she made her Come Out. With her betrothed, a powerful duke breaking it off to wed her sister, she's become the *tons* favorite piece of gossip. Never again wanting to experience the pain of a broken heart, she's resolved to make a match with a polite, respectable gentleman. The last thing she wants is another reckless rogue.

Lord Alex Edgerton has a problem. His brother, tired of Alex's carousing has charged him with chaperoning their remaining, unwed sister about *ton* events. Shopping? No, thank you. Attending the theatre? He'd rather be at Forbidden Pleasures with a scantily clad beauty upon his lap. The task of *chaperone* becomes even more of a bother when his sister drags along her dearest friend, Lady Imogen to social functions. The last thing he wants in his life is a young, innocent English miss.

Except, as Alex and Imogen are thrown together, passions flare and Alex comes to find he not only wants Imogen in his bed, but also in his heart. Yet now he must convince Imogen to risk all, on the heart of a rogue.

MORE THAN A DUKE
Book 2 in the "Heart of a Duke" Series by Christi Caldwell

Polite Society doesn't take Lady Anne Adamson seriously. However, Anne isn't just another pretty young miss. When she discovers her father betrayed her mother's love and her family descended into poverty, Anne comes up with a plan to marry a respectable, powerful, and honorable gentleman—a man nothing like her philandering father.

Armed with the heart of a duke pendant, fabled to land the wearer a duke's heart, she decides to enlist the aid of the notorious Harry, 6th Earl of Stanhope. A scoundrel with a scandalous past, he is the last gentleman she'd ever wed…however, his reputation marks him the perfect man to school her in the art of seduction so she might ensnare the illustrious Duke of Crawford.

Harry, the Earl of Stanhope is a jaded, cynical rogue who lives for his own pleasures. Having been thrown over by the only woman he ever loved so she could wed a duke, he's not at all surprised when Lady Anne approaches him with her scheme to capture another duke's affection. He's come to appreciate that all women are in fact greedy, title-grasping, self-indulgent creatures. And with Anne's history of grating on his every last nerve, she is the last woman he'd ever agree to school in the art of seduction. Only his friendship with the lady's sister compels him to help.

What begins as a pretend courtship, born of lessons on seduction, becomes something more leaving Anne to decide if she can give her heart to a reckless rogue, and Harry must decide if he's willing to again trust in a lady's love.

FOR LOVE OF THE DUKE
First Full-Length Book in the "Heart of a Duke" Series
by Christi Caldwell

After the tragic death of his wife, Jasper, the 8th Duke of Bainbridge buried himself away in the dark cold walls of his home, Castle Blackwood. When he's coaxed out of his self-imposed exile to attend the amusements of the Frost Fair, his life is irrevocably changed by his fateful meeting with Lady Katherine Adamson.

With her tight brown ringlets and silly white-ruffled gowns, Lady Katherine Adamson has found her dance card empty for two Seasons. After her father's passing, Katherine learned the unreliability of men, and is determined to depend on no one, except herself. Until she meets Jasper…

In a desperate bid to avoid a match arranged by her family, Katherine makes the Duke of Bainbridge a shocking proposition—one that he accepts.

Only, as Katherine begins to love Jasper, she finds the arrangement agreed upon is not enough. And Jasper is left to decide if protecting his heart is more important than fighting for Katherine's love.

IN NEED OF A DUKE
A Prequel Novella to "The Heart of a Duke" Series
by Christi Caldwell

In Need of a Duke: (Author's Note: This is a prequel novella to "The Heart of a Duke" series by Christi Caldwell. It was originally available in "The Heart of a Duke" Collection and is now being published as an individual novella.

~★~

It features a new prologue and epilogue.

Years earlier, a gypsy woman passed to Lady Aldora Adamson and her friends a heart pendant that promised them each the heart of a duke.

Now, a young lady, with her family facing ruin and scandal, Lady Aldora doesn't have time for mythical stories about cheap baubles. She needs to save her sisters and brother by marrying a titled gentleman with wealth and power to his name. She sets her bespectacled sights upon the Marquess of St. James.

Turned out by his father after a tragic scandal, Lord Michael Knightly has grown into a powerful, but self-made man. With the whispers and stares that still follow him, he would rather be anywhere but London…

Until he meets Lady Aldora, a young woman who mistakes him for his brother, the Marquess of St. James. The connection between Aldora and Michael is immediate and as they come to know one another, Aldora's feelings for Michael war with her sisterly responsibilities. With her family's dire situation, a man of Michael's scandalous past will never do.

Ultimately, Aldora must choose between her responsibilities as a sister and her love for Michael.

ONCE A WALLFLOWER, AT LAST HIS LOVE
Book 6 in the Scandalous Seasons Series

Responsible, practical Miss Hermione Rogers, has been crafting stories as the notorious Mr. Michael Michaelmas and selling them for a meager wage to support her siblings. The only real way to ensure her family's ruinous debts are paid, however, is to marry. Tall, thin, and plain, she has no expectation of success. In London for her first Season she seizes the chance to write the tale of a brooding duke. In her research, she finds Sebastian Fitzhugh, the 5th Duke of Mallen, who unfortunately is perfectly affable, charming, and so nicely… configured… he takes her breath away. He lacks all the character traits she needs for her story, but alas, any duke will have to do.

Sebastian Fitzhugh, the 5th Duke of Mallen has been deceived so many times during the high-stakes game of courtship, he's lost faith in Society women. Yet, after a chance encounter with Hermione, he finds himself intrigued. Not a woman he'd normally consider beautiful, the young lady's practical bent, her forthright nature and her tendency to turn up in the oddest places has his interests... roused. He'd like to trust her, he'd like to do a whole lot more with her too, but should he?

A Marquess For Christmas
Book 5 in the Scandalous Seasons Series

Lady Patrina Tidemore gave up on the ridiculous notion of true love after having her heart shattered and her trust destroyed by a black-hearted cad. Used as a pawn in a game of revenge against her brother, Patrina returns to London from a failed elopement with a tattered reputation and little hope for a respectable match. The only peace she finds is in her solitude on the cold winter days at Hyde Park. And even that is yanked from her by two little hellions who just happen to have a devastatingly handsome, but coldly aloof father, the Marquess of Beaufort. Something about the lord stirs the dreams she'd once carried for an honorable gentleman's love.

Weston Aldridge, the 4th Marquess of Beaufort was deceived and betrayed by his late wife. In her faithlessness, he's come to view women as self-serving, indulgent creatures. Except, after a series of chance encounters with Patrina, he comes to appreciate how uniquely different she is than all women he's ever known.

At the Christmastide season, a time of hope and new beginnings, Patrina and Weston, unexpectedly learn true love in one another. However, as Patrina's scandalous past threatens their future and the happiness of his children, they are both left to determine if love is enough.

ALWAYS A ROGUE, FOREVER HER LOVE
Book 4 in the Scandalous Seasons Series

Miss Juliet Marshville is spitting mad. With one guardian missing, and the other singularly uninterested in her fate, she is at the mercy of her wastrel brother who loses her beloved childhood home to a man known as Sin. Determined to reclaim control of Rosecliff Cottage and her own fate, Juliet arranges a meeting with the notorious rogue and demands the return of her property.

Jonathan Tidemore, 5th Earl of Sinclair, known to the *ton* as Sin, is exceptionally lucky in life and at the gaming tables. He has just one problem. Well…four, really. His incorrigible sisters have driven off yet another governess. This time, however, his mother demands he find an appropriate replacement.

When Miss Juliet Marshville boldly demands the return of her precious cottage, he takes advantage of his sudden good fortune and puts an offer to her; turn his sisters into proper English ladies, and he'll return Rosecliff Cottage to Juliet's possession.

Jonathan comes to appreciate Juliet's spirit, courage, and clever wit, and decides to claim the fiery beauty as his mistress. Juliet, however, will be mistress for no man. Nor could she ever love a man who callously stole her home in a game of cards. As Jonathan begins to see Juliet as more than a spirited beauty to warm his bed, he realizes she could be a lady he could love the rest of his life, if only he can convince the proud Juliet that he's worthy of her hand and heart.

ALWAYS PROPER, SUDDENLY SCANDALOUS
Book 3 in the Scandalous Seasons Series

Geoffrey Winters, Viscount Redbrooke was not always the hard, unrelenting lord driven by propriety. After a tragic mistake, he resolved to honor his responsibility to the Redbrooke line and live a life, free of scandal. Knowing his duty is to wed a proper, respectable English miss, he selects Lady Beatrice Dennington, daughter of the Duke of Somerset, the perfect woman for him. Until he meets Miss Abigail Stone...

To distance herself from a personal scandal, Abigail Stone flees America to visit her uncle, the Duke of Somerset. Determined to never trust a man again, she is helplessly intrigued by the hard, too-proper Geoffrey. With his strict appreciation for decorum and order, he is nothing like the man' she's always dreamed of.

Abigail is everything Geoffrey does not need. She upends his carefully ordered world at every encounter. As they begin to care for one another, Abigail carefully guards the secret that resulted in her journey to England.

Only, if Geoffrey learns the truth about Abigail, he must decide which he holds most dear: his place in Society or Abigail's place in his heart.

NEVER COURTED, SUDDENLY WED
Book 2 in the Scandalous Seasons Series

Christopher Ansley, Earl of Waxham, has constructed a perfect image for the *ton*—the ladies love him and his company is desired by all. Only two people know the truth about Waxham's secret. Unfortunately, one of them is Miss Sophie Winters.

Sophie Winters has known Christopher since she was in leading strings. As children, they delighted in tormenting each other. Now at two and twenty, she still has a tendency to find herself in scrapes, and her marital prospects are slim.

When his father threatens to expose his shame to the *ton*, unless he weds Sophie for her dowry, Christopher concocts a plan to remain a bachelor. What he didn't plan on was falling in love with the lively, impetuous Sophie. As secrets are exposed, will Christopher's love be enough when she discovers his role in his father's scheme?

Forever Betrothed, Never the Bride
Book 1 in the Scandalous Seasons Series

Hopeless romantic Lady Emmaline Fitzhugh is tired of sitting with the wallflowers, waiting for her betrothed to come to his senses and marry her. When Emmaline reads one too many reports of his scandalous liaisons in the gossip rags, she takes matters into her own hands.

War-torn veteran Lord Drake devotes himself to forgetting his days on the Peninsula through an endless round of meaningless associations. He no longer wants to feel anything, but Lady Emmaline is making it hard to maintain a state of numbness. With her zest for life, she awakens his passion and desire for love.

The one woman Drake has spent the better part of his life avoiding is now the only woman he needs, but he is no longer a man worthy of his Emmaline. It is up to her to show him the healing power of love.

A Season of Hope
A Danby Novella

Five years ago when her love, Marcus Wheatley, failed to return from fighting Napoleon's forces, Lady Olivia Foster buried her heart. Unable to betray Marcus's memory, Olivia has gone out of her way to run off prospective suitors. At three and twenty she considers herself firmly on the shelf. Her father, however, disagrees and accepts an offer for Olivia's hand in marriage. Yet it's Christmas, when anything can happen…

Olivia receives a well-timed summons from her grandfather, the Duke of Danby, and eagerly embraces the reprieve from her betrothal.

Only, when Olivia arrives at Danby Castle she realizes the Christmas season represents hope, second chances, and even miracles.

"WINNING A LADY'S HEART"
A Danby Novella

Author's Note: This is a novella that was originally available in A Summons From The Castle (The Regency Christmas Summons Collection). It is being published as an individual novella.

~★~

For Lady Alexandra, being the source of a cold, calculated wager is bad enough…but when it is waged by Nathaniel Michael Winters, 5th Earl of Pembroke, the man she's in love with, it results in a broken heart, the scandal of the season, and a summons from her grandfather – the Duke of Danby.

To escape Society's gossip, she hurries to her meeting with the duke, determined to put memories of the earl far behind. Except the duke has other plans for Alexandra…plans which include the 5th Earl of Pembroke!

TEMPTED BY A LADY'S SMILE
Book 4 in the "Lords of Honor" Series

Richard Jonas has loved but one woman—a woman who belongs to his brother. Refusing to suffer any longer, he evades his family in order to barricade his heart from unrequited love. While attending a friend's summer party, Richard's approach to love is changed after sharing a passionate and life-altering kiss with a vibrant and mysterious woman. Believing he was incapable of loving again, Richard finds himself tempted by a young lady determined to marry his best friend.

Gemma Reed has not been treated kindly by the *ton*. Often disregarded for her appearance and interests unlike those of a proper lady, Gemma heads to house party to win the heart of Lord Westfield, the man she's loved for years. But her plan is set off course by the tempting and intriguing, Richard Jonas.

A chance meeting creates a new path for Richard and Gemma to forage—but can two people, scorned and shunned by those they've loved from afar, let down their guards to find true happiness?

"Rescued By A Lady's Love"
Book 3 in the "Lords of Honor" Series

Destitute and determined to finally be free of any man's shackles, Lily Benedict sets out to salvage her honor. With no choice but to commit a crime that will save her from her past, she enters the home of the recluse, Derek Winters, the new Duke of Blackthorne. But entering the "Beast of Blackthorne's" lair proves more threatening than she ever imagined.

With half a face and a mangled leg, Derek—once rugged and charming—only exists within the confines of his home. Shunned by society, Derek is leery of the hauntingly beautiful Lily Benedict. As time passes, she slips past his defenses, reminding him how to live again. But when Lily's sordid past comes back, threatening her life, it's up to Derek to find the strength to become the hero he once was. Can they overcome the darkness of their sins to find a life of love and redemption?

Captivated by a Lady's Charm
Book 2 in the "Lords of Honor" Series

In need of a wife...

Christian Villiers, the Marquess of St. Cyr, despises the role he's been cast into as fortune hunter but requires the funds to keep his marquisate solvent. Yet, the sins of his past cloud his future, preventing him from seeing beyond his fateful actions at the Battle of Toulouse. For he knows inevitably it will catch up with him, and everyone will remember his actions on the battlefield that cost so many so much—particularly his best friend.

In want of a husband…

Lady Prudence Tidemore's life is plagued by familial scandals, which makes her own marital prospects rather grim. Surely there is one gentleman of the ton who can look past her family and see just her and all she has to offer?

When Prudence runs into Christian on a London street, the charming, roguish gentleman immediately captures her attention. But then a chance meeting becomes a waltz, and now…

A Perfect Match…

All she must do is convince Christian to forget the cold requirements he has for his future marchioness. But the demons in his past prevent him from turning himself over to love. One thing is certain—Prudence wants the marquess and is determined to have him in her life, now and forever. It's just a matter of convincing Christian he wants the same.

ᏚEDUCED ᏰY A ᏞADY'S ᏞEART
Book 1 in the "Lords of Honor" Series

You met Lieutenant Lucien Jones in "Forever Betrothed, Never the Bride" when he was a broken soldier returned from fighting Boney's forces. This is his story of triumph and happily-ever-after!

∼★∼

Lieutenant Lucien Jones, son of a viscount, returned from war, to find his wife and child dead. Blaming his father for the commission that sent him off to fight Boney's forces, he was content to languish at London Hospital… until offered employment on the Marquess of Drake's staff. Through his position, Lucien found purpose in life and is content to keep his past buried.

Lady Eloise Yardley has loved Lucien since they were children. Having long ago given up on the dream of him, she married another. Years later, she is a young, lonely widow who does not fit in with the ton. When Lucien's family enlists her aid to reunite father and son, she leaps at the opportunity to not only aid her former friend, but to also escape London.

Lucien doesn't know what scheme Eloise has concocted, but

knowing her as he does, when she pays a visit to his employer, he knows she's up to something. The last thing he wants is the temptation that this new, older, mature Eloise presents; a tantalizing reminder of happier times and peace.

Yet Eloise is determined to win Lucien's love once and for all... if only Lucien can set aside the pain of his past and risk all on a lady's heart.

Only For Their Love
Book 3 in the "The Theodosia Sword" Series

Miss Carol Cresswall bore witness to her parents' loveless union and is determined to avoid that same miserable fate. Her mother has altogether different plans—plans that include a match between Carol and Lord Gregory Renshaw. Despite his wealth and power, Carol has no interest in marrying a pompous man who goes out of his way to ignore her. Now, with their families coming together for the Christmastide season it's her mother's last-ditch effort to get them together. And Carol plans to avoid Gregory at all costs.

Lord Gregory Renshaw has no intentions of falling prey to his mother's schemes to marry him off to a proper debutante she's picked out. Over the years, he has carefully sidestepped all endeavors to be matched with any of the grasping ladies.

But a sudden Christmastide Scandal has the potential show Carol and Gregory that they've spent years running from the one thing they've always needed.

ONLY FOR HER HONOR
Book 2 in the "The Theodosia Sword" Series

A wounded soldier:

When Captain Lucas Rayne returned from fighting Boney's forces, he was a shell of a man. A recluse who doesn't leave his family's estate, he's content to shut himself away. Until he meets Eve…

A woman alone in the world:

Eve Ormond spent most of her life following the drum alongside her late father. When his shameful actions bring death and pain to English soldiers, Eve is forced back to England, an outcast. With no family or marital prospects she needs employment and finds it in Captain Lucas Rayne's home. A man whose life was ruined by her father, Eve has no place inside his household. With few options available, however, Eve takes the post. What she never anticipates is how with their every meeting, this honorable, hurting soldier slips inside her heart.

The Secrets Between Them:

The more time Lucas spends with Eve, he remembers what it is to be alive and he lets the walls protecting his heart down. When the secrets between them come to light will their love be enough? Or are they two destined for heartbreak?

ONLY FOR HIS LADY
Book 1 in the "The Theodosia Sword" Series

A curse. A sword. And the thief who stole her heart.

The Rayne family is trapped in a rut of bad luck. And now, it's up to Lady Theodosia Rayne to steal back the Theodosia sword, a gladius that was pilfered by the rival, loathed Renshaw family. Hopefully, recovering the stolen sword will break the cycle and reverse her family's fate.

Damian Renshaw, the Duke of Devlin, is feared by all—all, that is, except Lady Theodosia, the brazen spitfire who enters his home and wrestles an ancient relic from his wall. Intrigued by the vivacious woman, Devlin has no intentions of relinquishing the sword to her.

As Theodosia and Damian battle for ownership, passion ignites. Now, they are torn between their age-old feud and the fire that burns between them. Can two forbidden lovers find a way to make amends before their families' war tears them apart?

My Lady of Deception
Book 1 in the "Brethren of the Lords" Series

This dark, sweeping Regency novel was previously only offered as part of the limited edition box sets: "From the Ballroom and Beyond", "Romancing the Rogue", and "Dark Deceptions". Now, available for the first time on its own, exclusively through Amazon is "My Lady of Deception".

~★~

Everybody has a secret. Some are more dangerous than others.

For Georgina Wilcox, only child of the notorious traitor known as "The Fox", there are too many secrets to count. However, after her interference results in great tragedy, she resolves to never help another... until she meets Adam Markham.

Lord Adam Markham is captured by The Fox. Imprisoned, Adam loses everything he holds dear. As his days in captivity grow, he finds himself fascinated by the young maid, Georgina, who cares for him.

When the carefully crafted lies she's built between them begin to crumble, Georgina realizes she will do anything to prove her love and loyalty to Adam—even it means at the expense of her own life.

NON-FICTION WORKS BY
CHRISTI CALDWELL

**Uninterrupted Joy: Memoir: My Journey through
Infertility, Pregnancy, and Special Needs**

The following journey was never intended for publication.
It was written from a mother, to her unborn child. The words
detailed her struggle through infertility and the joy of finally being
pregnant. A stunning revelation at her son's birth opened a world
of both fear and discovery. This is the story of one mother's love
and hope and…her quest for uninterrupted joy.

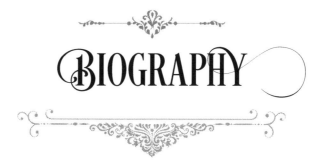

BIOGRAPHY

Christi Caldwell is the bestselling author of historical romance novels set in the Regency era. Christi blames Judith McNaught's "Whitney, My Love," for luring her into the world of historical romance. While sitting in her graduate school apartment at the University of Connecticut, Christi decided to set aside her notes and try her hand at writing romance. She believes the most perfect heroes and heroines have imperfections and rather enjoys tormenting them before crafting a well-deserved happily ever after!

When Christi isn't writing the stories of flawed heroes and heroines, she can be found in her Southern Connecticut home chasing around her eight-year-old son, and caring for twin princesses-in-training!

Visit *www.christicaldwellauthor.com* to learn more about what Christi is working on, or join her on Facebook at Christi Caldwell Author, and Twitter *@ChristiCaldwell*

63091867R00086

Made in the USA
Middletown, DE
29 January 2018